Sparrow
Being
Sparrow

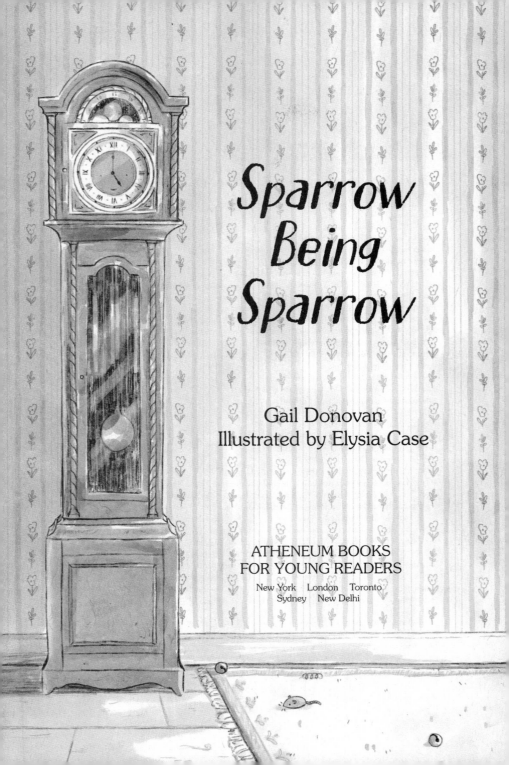

Sparrow Being Sparrow

Gail Donovan
Illustrated by Elysia Case

ATHENEUM BOOKS
FOR YOUNG READERS
New York   London   Toronto
Sydney   New Delhi

ATHENEUM BOOKS FOR YOUNG READERS
An imprint of Simon & Schuster Children's Publishing Division
1230 Avenue of the Americas, New York, New York 10020

Text © 2023 by Gail Donovan
Jacket illustration © 2023 by Elysia Case
Jacket design by Karyn Lee © 2023 by Simon & Schuster, Inc.
Interior illustration © 2023 by Elysia Case

For information about special discounts for bulk purchases, please contact Simon & Schuster Special Sales at 1-866-506-1949 or business@simonandschuster.com.
The Simon & Schuster Speakers Bureau can bring authors to your live event. For more information or to book an event, contact the Simon & Schuster Speakers Bureau at 1-866-248-3049 or visit our website at www.simonspeakers.com.
Interior design by Karyn Lee
The text for this book was set in Cotford Text.
The illustrations for this book were rendered digitally.
Manufactured in the United States of America
0623 FFG
First Edition
10 9 8 7 6 5 4 3 2 1
Library of Congress Cataloging-in-Publication Data
Names: Donovan, Gail, 1962- author.
Title: Sparrow being Sparrow / Gail Donovan.
Description: First edition. | New York : Atheneum Books for Young Readers, [2023] | Audience: Ages 7–10. | Audience: Grades 4–6. | Summary: Nine-year-old Sparrow Robinson blames herself for her elderly neighbor's accident, so she promises to take care of Mrs. LaRose's seven cats, all while trying to adjust to a new school—but things become complicated when she has to find new homes for all of the cats plus some unexpected kittens.
Identifiers: LCCN 2022006119 (print) | LCCN 2022006120 (ebook) | ISBN 9781665916691 (hardcover) | ISBN 9781665916714 (ebook)
Subjects: LCSH: Cats—Juvenile fiction. | Kittens—Juvenile fiction. | Responsibility—Juvenile fiction. | Helping behavior—Juvenile fiction. | Neighbors—Juvenile fiction. | Friendship—Juvenile fiction. | Elementary schools—Juvenile fiction. | CYAC: Cats—Fiction. | Responsibility—Fiction. | Helpfulness—Fiction. | Neighbors—Fiction. | Friendship—Fiction. | Elementary schools—Fiction. | Schools—Fiction.
Classification: LCC PZ7.D7227 Sp 2023 (print) | LCC PZ7.D7227 (ebook) | DDC 813.6 [Fic]—dc23/eng/20220524
LC record available at https://lccn.loc.gov/2022006119
LC ebook record available at https://lccn.loc.gov/2022006120

For Mary-Alice, who took a chance on me
—G. D.

To my mom—for all the books, cats, and art
—E. C.

⤜ 1 ⤝

*S*parrow. *Sparrow!* SPARROW!

That was how the sirens sounded. First far away, like someone whispering. Then getting closer. Louder. Like someone scolding: *Sparrow. Sparrow! SPARROW! Your fault. Your fault! YOUR FAULT!*

Sparrow knelt beside Mrs. LaRose. The sound of the sirens was so much bigger than everything else.

Everything else was this: Mrs. LaRose on the green grass. Under the blue sky. And a white cat, bumping its head against the old lady's hand, asking to be petted.

Mrs. LaRose was trying to say something, but Sparrow couldn't hear because the sirens were so crazy loud. *See? See? See? See what happens when you get carried away?*

Now the ambulance came screeching down the

street, with a fire truck right behind it, red lights flashing. They pulled up in front of the house, and the sirens finally stopped. In the silence Sparrow heard Mrs. LaRose.

"My cats," she said.

"Don't worry about the cats," said Sparrow. "I'll take care of them. I promise."

She didn't know what "them" meant, exactly. Mrs. LaRose had a lot of cats. But some were shy and hid whenever Sparrow came by. And some were outside cats that weren't always around. She *did* know that no matter how many cats Mrs. LaRose had, she'd take care of them. For one thing, she had promised.

And for another thing, this was all her fault.

⤜ 2 ⤛

Alone, Sparrow sat on the grass, next to the spot where Mrs. LaRose had lain. Poor Mrs. LaRose! What if she wasn't okay? What if . . . Sparrow couldn't even think about the worst "what if."

Then the white cat—which had slunk off while the ambulance crew was putting Mrs. LaRose on a stretcher and taking her away—came back and began butting its head against Sparrow's hand. *Pet me.*

"Hello, Mrs. Moon," said Sparrow, stroking the cat's soft white fur, and wondered, *Where are all the other cats?* She had asked Mrs. LaRose once how many cats she had. The answer was *"Ne demande pas."* In English: "Don't ask." So Sparrow didn't know.

There was a lot more Sparrow didn't know. In fact, there was way more that she *didn't* know than she *did*.

Here was what she knew about Mrs. LaRose.

One: she didn't like questions. Two: she owned the house Sparrow and her family had moved into that summer. She lived in one half of the house, and Sparrow lived in the other half with her mom and dad. And three: she cared about all kinds of animals. She'd been as excited as Sparrow when they found the monarch butterfly emerging from its chrysalis.

Unfortunately, when Sparrow got excited, things tended to go wrong.

↘ 3 ↙

Barefoot, Sparrow padded across the grass, with Mrs. Moon slinking along beside her. She went up the porch steps and opened Mrs. LaRose's front door. She felt weird. Taking care of the cats meant she should feed them, and feeding them meant going inside. But she had never been in Mrs. LaRose's unit all by herself. It felt different, all alone.

Sparrow had seen shows about traveling back in time, and Mrs. LaRose's place felt like that. Frozen in another time. In the hallway stood a giant clock with hands that went around in a circle, ticking off the minutes and gonging every hour. *Gong! Gong! Gong!* at three o'clock. Seven gongs at seven.

The kitchen smelled like lemons. Stuck to the wall was an old-fashioned landline telephone with a long, twisty cord. There were old-looking chairs circling an old-looking table. In the middle of the table was what Mrs. LaRose called a lazy Susan, a plate that circled around so somebody could more easily reach what was on it—salt and pepper shakers and a sugar bowl. The salt shaker was a white cat and the pepper shaker was a black cat, and the sugar bowl was in the shape of a cat's head, with ears on the lid and a tiny silver spoon.

Sparrow had a sweet tooth. And she loved the adorable sugar bowl with its special spoon. She had been wanting to scoop up a spoonful of sugar from that sugar bowl ever since the first day she'd come in here. The day she had met Mrs. LaRose and her cats.

⤺ 4 ⤻

That day had been so hot. The announcer on the radio said it was the hottest day ever recorded in the state of Maine. But Sparrow didn't need anyone telling her it was crazy hot. She knew because the air-conditioning in the car was broken.

"It's so hot," she groaned.

Her legs felt glued to the seat of the car. It felt like when she used rubber cement in art class and her fingertips would get stuck together. Sparrow did not like that feeling. Sticky fingertips in art class was bad enough, but sticky legs on a long car ride was torture.

"It's the hottest day in the history of the world. I'm *dying.*"

"Your Majesty," said her father. "Oh Queen of Drama. Can you dial back the theatrics?"

"I'm not being a drama queen! That guy said it was the hottest day in Maine, *ever*."

"Yes, but Maine is not the hottest place in the world," said her dad, who was a stickler for facts. His whole job at the newspaper where he worked was checking people's facts. But Sparrow wished he weren't always fact-checking her, too. "So the hottest day here is not the hottest day in the whole history of the world."

"Dan, please," said Sparrow's mom. "Let's not go there."

Sparrow's mom said that a lot. Sparrow wasn't exactly sure where "there" was. Only that it had to do with her. "There" was like "the land of arguing with Sparrow." Sparrow didn't want to argue. But she didn't want to be ignored, either.

"Why did we have to move *today*?"

"Please don't be such a grumpus, Sparrow," said her mom. "We're moving today because it's the day we're moving," which Sparrow didn't think was much of an answer. It was like saying the sky is blue because it's blue. "It's going to be great. And we're *all* hot."

Being told not to be a grumpus drama queen, and being told how great everything was going to be, only made Sparrow grumpier. They were moving to a new house, and she would be going to a new school and would have to make all new friends. It might be great. Or it might not. But Sparrow did not like being told it would be great, like she wasn't even allowed to make up her own mind.

"This is it," said her dad, pulling into the driveway of a two-family house. "This is home."

The house was white, with a long, low porch across the front and two front doors painted dark green right next to each other. There was a lady standing on the porch, with braids as white as the house wound around her head.

"Let me out of here!" cried Sparrow. Her legs made a squelching noise as she unstuck them and sprang from the car.

"Be-ahn-va-noo," called the lady on the porch.

"That's Mrs. LaRose," explained Sparrow's mom. "*Bienvenue* means 'welcome.'"

"It's so hot," called Mrs. LaRose. "Come have something cold to drink, before you unpack your things."

Inside the house there were cats everywhere. Some scattered while others stayed put. A tabby cat sat on a wide windowsill, in between two pots of geraniums. A black cat was draped across the back of a comfy chair. And a white cat twined around Mrs. LaRose's legs as she took a pitcher from the refrigerator and poured out four glasses of lemonade.

"How many cats do you have?" blurted Sparrow. "Are you a cat lady?"

"*Sparrow!*" scolded her mom and dad in unison.

But Mrs. LaRose just laughed, giving a *Don't worry about it* wave of her hand. Then she lifted the top of the sugar bowl and scooped up a spoonful of sugar. She poured it into one of the glasses, stirred, and handed that one to Sparrow.

"Ne demande pas," she said.

"What's *that*?" cried Sparrow. She liked the way the words sounded, but she didn't know what they meant.

"*That*," said her mom, "is French. And it means 'Don't ask.'"

⚴ 5 ⚴

That was in August. Now it was September. Tomorrow was the first day of school. But the weather didn't feel like back-to-school weather. It was still summer-hot, barefoot weather.

Barefoot, Sparrow stepped across the kitchen, Mrs. Moon still at her heels. She sat down in one of the chairs circling the table and spun the lazy Susan around until the bowl of sugar was right in front of her. Then she scooped up a spoonful of sugar. The spoon was halfway to her mouth when the clock in the hallway sounded—*Gong!* Mrs. Moon jumped onto Sparrow's lap, knocking the spoon right out of her hand. Sugar scattered everywhere.

Another toll of the clock—*Gong!*—and another cat sprang from the comfy chair onto the table.

Gong! Another cat leapt down from the windowsill.

Gong! Two more cats streamed into the kitchen from wherever they had been in the house.

Gong! Another pair came to the screen door and started scratching to come in.

The gonging stopped and Mrs. Moon began butting her head against Sparrow's hand.

"Okay, I get it," said Sparrow. "Time for your supper."

Sparrow got it. Five gongs meant it was five o'clock. That must be when the cats were fed. But there was something she didn't get. Since they had moved here, she had been spending afternoons with Mrs. LaRose. It was just for an hour—the hour between when her dad left for work and her mom got home from work. But she had never been here before when the cats were getting fed. Which must mean that her mom was always home by five o'clock. So where was she today? How come she was late?

Mrs. Moon butted her head against Sparrow's hand again, as if she were saying, *Never mind your mom. Feed me!*

Getting up to let in the outdoor cats, Sparrow felt spilled sugar under her bare feet. Now every step she took was a grainy sugar-step. She had to never mind that, too, because now the meowing cats were pacing to and fro around a cupboard door. She opened the door to find cans and cans and cans of cat food, all stacked

in neat rows. There was a stack of saucers, too, like the kind that went under a teacup.

Sparrow began opening one can after another, scooping the food onto a saucer, and setting each saucer on the floor. One by one, each cat claimed a saucer. One. Two. Three. Four. Five. Six. Seven. So now she knew: there were seven cats. She realized she knew all their names too. She had seen all of them at one time or another, just not all at once.

The white cat was Mrs. Moon.

The all-black cat was Midnight, and the black cat with a white throat was Tux, short for Tuxedo.

The brown-and-black tabby was Pierre, the tabby with the white paws was Paulette, and the orange tabby was Marmalade.

Lastly, there was a gray cat called Kitty Gray.

Seven cats. Could Sparrow really take care of seven cats? What about tomorrow? Would the cats be okay while she was in school? Questions were twirling around in her head, asking to be answered, the way Mrs. Moon twined around her ankles, asking to be petted. Suddenly the big black phone hanging on the wall began ringing. *Answer! Answer! Answer!*

Sparrow didn't answer. She bolted.

⚡ 6 ⚡

"**H**ey, sweetie!" said Sparrow's mom. "Sorry I'm late. I had a doctor's appointment after work, and they were running behind. I called to let Mrs. LaRose know, but nobody picked up. And I called just now to say I was home, but nobody picked up again. Everything okay?"

Instead of answering, Sparrow went in for a hug. Inside the circle of her mom's arms, she could feel her heart pounding, the way her feet had pounded across the front porch, running from Mrs. LaRose's side of the house to their side. She knew her heart was always beating, but it was weird to *feel* it. Pound, pound, pound.

"Sparrow, you okay?" repeated her mom, holding her tight.

Too tight. Sparrow wriggled out of her mom's hug and gave a quick *okay* nod. She loved hugs, but not long ones. Long hugs made her feel squished, and squished was one of her least favorite feelings. It was worse than sticky.

"Well, how was your day?" asked her mom.

Sparrow's day had started out normal. Normal right now was hanging out with her dad until he left for work, then being babysat—except she hated that word, nine years old wasn't a baby—by Mrs. LaRose until her mom got home.

Her mom worked days in a dentist's office, fixing people's teeth. Her dad worked nights at the news-paper, fixing people's writing. They both said that everyone makes mistakes. But Sparrow was pretty sure they both thought it was better to do things right in the first place. Brush your teeth and get your facts straight.

Sparrow's mom said, "Did you hear me, sweetie? I asked how your day was."

Normal, thought Sparrow. *Except for the part where Mrs. LaRose got taken away in an ambulance.*

"Normal," she said.

"Well, my day was pretty fun because guess what? I got a call from your teacher, and she sounded really nice. She wanted to touch base and see if I had any questions. I asked if she was ready for a great kid who could be a *little* high spirited. So—did you decide what you're wearing tomorrow?"

Sparrow shook her head. "I'm not going."

"What? Where did this come from? I thought you were excited to start school."

"I changed my mind," said Sparrow. "I'm not going. I can't!"

Sparrow's mom had a puzzled look on her face. "What do you mean, 'can't'?"

Sparrow couldn't go to school because now she had to stay home to take care of the cats. Which she needed to explain to her mom. But explaining about the cats meant explaining about Mrs. LaRose. Which made her heart feel poundy again. How could she not be in major trouble?

"I just can't," she said.

"Well," said her mom, "we can talk about you feeling like you don't *want* to go. But you *are* going. That's not up for debate, so let's not go there."

"I'm not *going anywhere*," said Sparrow.

This wasn't how she wanted the conversation to go. Fighting with her mom until it all came out. But that was how conversations usually went in her family.

Until this summer. Her parents had taken a class on "positive parenting," and now they had different "strategies."

"You know," said her mom, "I bet we're both hungry.

So let's put a pin in that and talk again after supper."
She began rummaging in the refrigerator. "It's so hot, I
think we'll have a big salad."

That was the "not engaging" strategy. Otherwise
known as ignoring Sparrow. Which was probably a good
thing right now. But it still bugged her.

The whole "positive parenting" thing was supposed to be about discouraging the things they didn't
like and encouraging the stuff they liked. But as far
as Sparrow could tell, all they saw was the didn't-like
stuff. The too-much stuff. Too much drama. Too much
shouting instead of using her "inside voice." Too much
running and climbing and dancing around, instead of
walking or, better yet, sitting still in a chair.

She stepped up onto one of the
kitchen chairs. Then she hopped
from that chair to another. She
made her way around the table,
chair to chair. She was a bird flit-
ting from branch to branch. One,
two, three, four. There were

three of them in the family—her, her mom, and her dad. The fourth chair was extra.

Sparrow's mom closed the fridge door and turned around. "Sparrow, get down from there!" she cried. "That was cute when you were little, but you're too big for that now!"

Sparrow hopped down, to show she was "listening and responding." Which was the rule. Then she added a little twirl at the end of the hop, to show that even if she had to follow the rules, her mom wasn't the boss of her.

Her mom took a can of cold seltzer from the fridge and held it to her cheek. "Let's review," she said. "You're constantly leaping and jumping and flying all over the house, but you don't want to take a dance class."

Sparrow shook her head. "Nope."

"Or gymnastics, or any kind of sport."

"Nope."

"Or drama, even though you'd be *amazing*."

"Nope."

"You just want to come home after school."

Sparrow nodded. "Yep."

Her mom popped the top of the can and took a long swig. "I get that," she said. "I used to love coming home after school too. But I hope you know how lucky you are, that between Daddy's and my schedules, that works out. It was incredibly nice of Mrs. LaRose to say you could come over every day, for the hour after Daddy leaves and before I get back."

"I know," said Sparrow.

"Well, I hope you don't stand on her chairs."

"Of course I don't!" cried Sparrow. She began to feel something building up inside her, getting bigger and bigger, like the sirens getting louder and louder.

"So, what do you two do every day?" asked her mom.

Sparrow didn't answer. Instead she burst into tears.

Just then her mom's phone buzzed. Her mom looked at Sparrow crying and then looked down at her phone.

"Who could be calling me from Maine Medical? Honey, I better take this." She answered, then held the phone to her ear and listened for a second. "Yes," she said. "This is Susan Robinson. Yes, I'm Mrs. LaRose's neighbor. What's happened?"

"Hey," said Sparrow's dad as his face popped up on the laptop screen, a big smile curving beneath his mustache. He used to have a beard, but this summer was so hot, he'd shaved off everything but the mustache. His face still looked funny to Sparrow, as if he weren't all there anymore.

"This is a nice surprise!" he said. "What's up?"

Sparrow and her mom shared the little box in one corner of the screen. People said Sparrow looked like her mom. They had the same reddish-brown freckles on pale skin, like cinnamon sprinkled on white bread. They had the same brown hair, which her mom wore pulled back with a scrunchie and Sparrow wore in two long braids.

"Sorry to bother you at work, hon," said Sparrow's

mom. "But I think we need to hear this together, and it can't wait."

On the screen, the curve of her dad's smile became a straight, serious line. "I'm listening," he said.

Sparrow's mom said, "I got a call from Jenny LaRose, Mrs. LaRose's daughter. She's in the hospital with a broken hip. Jenny said her mom wants to make sure we know—and I quote—'it wasn't Sparrow's fault.' Also, she asked us to take care of the cats for a few days."

"I already am!" interrupted Sparrow. "I said I would. I already gave them their supper and everything. I know where the food is, and I opened the cans. I can do it!"

"Let's hear the whole story, Sparrow," said her mom.

"We were in the yard," began Sparrow.

Bit by bit she tried to explain. They were really excited because of the chrysalis. It was on one of the plants in the garden. They had seen the caterpillar a while ago, and then the chrysalis forming, and then—today—it was hatching! And a monarch butterfly was coming out! Sparrow was talking faster now, trying to get the story out.

"So we were dancing," she said.

"Why does this not surprise me?" murmured her dad.

"We were doing, like, the dance of the butterflies."

It was hard to explain in words. She stood up and tried to show them.

"We were making believe we were flying to Mexico. I was leaping." She leapt to the left. "And Mrs. LaRose was leaping." She leapt to the right. "And then I guess we . . . crashed? And Mrs. LaRose fell down. And she couldn't get up."

Sparrow's mom said, "Let me get this straight. You broke Mrs. LaRose's hip by doing a make-believe monarch butterfly dance?"

Her dad had a funny, crooked smile on his face. "Sounds like Sparrow being Sparrow," he said.

Her mom asked, "And who called 911?"

"I did!"

"Well, that was a godsend," said her mom.

"What's a godsend?"

"It means you got a little help from your guardian angel," said her mom.

Sparrow didn't get why her accidentally breaking someone's hip was all on her, but her calling 911 was because she got some kind of extra help.

Her parents were both staring at her—her mom from right beside her, and her dad through the screen— with the same expression. Dazed and determined. Dazed because they couldn't believe what they had just heard. Determined because they were people who fixed mistakes. And somehow they would fix Sparrow, until she wasn't the kind of kid who got so carried away with her imagination that she could send an old lady to the hospital.

Until she wasn't such a drama queen.

Until she wasn't "Sparrow being Sparrow" anymore.

⤝ 8 ⤞

Sparrow was walking to the first day of school with her mom. Her legs were going in that direction, anyway. Her head was heading back to the house, wondering what the cats were doing.

Earlier that morning her dad had gone with her to feed them. They found seven hungry cats. Also, a trail of ants trekking across the floor, carrying away the spilled sugar. Also, some giant bluebottle flies buzzing around the empty cans Sparrow had left on the counter. Her dad had helped her clean everything up, and she had promised it wouldn't happen again. But all he had said was, "We'll see, Sparrow. It's a big job." Sparrow was not a fan of "we'll see." It usually meant grown-ups organizing things the way *they* wanted to see them.

"You remember the way, right?" asked her mom.

Sparrow nodded. "I remember," she said.

They had practiced last week. First—from their house, turn left and go down their street toward the corner.

The houses on Hartley Street were almost all like Mrs. LaRose's—two houses in one. Front yards with a square of grass. Driveways down the side. Sparrow and her mom passed one house where the yard was all fenced in. Hanging from the porch was a flag dotted with ladybugs and the word WELCOME!

Sparrow's legs were still going one way and her head another. "Mom, what about Mrs. LaRose? Is she okay?"

"Honey, listen. It was an accident. You didn't mean to hurt her—everybody knows that."

"But when will she come home?"

"I don't know."

"Can I go see her?"

"Sparrow, I'll see what I can find out, but for right now can you pay attention to where we're going? I took today and tomorrow off from work, partly so I could get some more boxes unpacked, but mostly so I could walk you to and from school and make sure you know the way. So this week is one thing, but next week . . ." Her mom broke off. "Actually, next week, who knows?"

"Who knows *what*?"

"Who knows if you'll even be walking by yourself?" said her mom.

"You already said I could! You said Daddy could walk me in the morning, if I want, but after school I could walk home by myself!"

"I know," said her mom. "But you won't be coming home after school—not anymore. With Mrs. LaRose gone, I'm not sure where you'll go. I need to make some calls, figure it out."

"Mom, I have to come home! I have to take care of the cats! I promised!"

"Sparrow, this is not the time for a big scene about the cats," said her mom. "It's time to pay attention to where you're going. Now, you remember what to do here?"

"Yes," said Sparrow. "This is where I turn."

At the end of Hartley, they turned onto Bridge Street, which was bigger. The sidewalk was wider, and some of the houses had been turned into businesses. Yummy smells came drifting out of a bakery, where people were sitting outside at tiny tables.

In another block they came to the place with a church on one side of the street and the public library on the other. This was where Sparrow was going to cross. She pushed the crosswalk button. Lights flashed, and cars slowed and then stopped. Sparrow looked in both directions. Left and right. Then both ways again. Then started across.

"Good job," said her mom.

In a little bit they turned onto the road that led to the school, and in a few minutes they were there. In front of the school, yellow buses stood in one spot, and in another spot cars were pulling up and letting kids out. Everywhere, people were streaming toward a single propped-open door. Beside the door stood a woman saying hello to everyone.

"Want me to come in with you?" asked her mom.

Sparrow saw little kids, like kindergartners, walking in with their mom or dad. Big kids were going in alone.

"No," she said. "I'm good." She gave her mom a quick hug and headed for the door.

"Welcome!" said the lady standing next to the door. "Hello, welcome, *bienvenidos, ahlan wa sahlan, bien-venue.*"

Bienvenue! That was how Mrs. LaRose said "welcome"!

Sparrow turned to wave goodbye to her mom. She spotted her standing next to some lady wearing a dress in Sparrow's favorite color—hot pink. Her mom was so busy talking that it took her a minute to see Sparrow. When she did, she gave Sparrow a big thumbs-up.

Sparrow gave a little wave back; then, gripping the straps of her backpack, she headed inside.

⤲ 9 ⤳

Sparrow scoped out the room, searching for her desk. The desks were all bunched into pods. She counted five pods, each with four desks. Four desks in a pod times five pods meant twenty kids altogether. Nineteen, not counting her.

Where was she supposed to sit? All the desks had name cards on them. But she didn't see SPARROW anywhere.

"Fourth graders," said the teacher, "please take your seats."

Kids scrambled for their seats until everyone was sitting except her. She was the only kid still standing up. Gripping the straps of her backpack, she went up to the teacher's desk. Mrs. Foxworthy had short, spiky hair topped with a pair of bright red eyeglasses, like a bird perched in a nest.

"I don't have a desk," said Sparrow.

"Oh no!" said Mrs. Foxworthy. She pulled her red-framed glasses down onto her nose and studied the paper on her clipboard. "You're not Sarah Robinson?"

Sarah was the name on the card at the empty desk. But Sarah was not *her* name. Sarah was the name she *used* to have, when she was a baby. She couldn't remember when her name changed, exactly. She couldn't even remember her grandfather. And she definitely couldn't remember him saying, "Are you a sparrow?" But that was the story her parents had told her, over and over. How she was always climbing on furniture and leaping down, making believe she could fly. Crying, "I'm flying!" How her grandpa always called her a sparrow. How the name had stuck.

"No," said Sparrow. "I'm Sparrow Robinson."

"Got it," said Mrs. Foxworthy, writing on her clipboard. "Sorry about that! Sarah Robinson—goes by Sparrow." Then she picked up the Sarah name card—a piece of oaktag folded in half—turned it inside out, and wrote *SPARROW* in big block letters on the other side.

Sparrow was about to say she didn't "go by" Sparrow. She *was* Sparrow. But just then a voice boomed *"Good morning"* over the intercom, and Mrs. Foxworthy smiled a no-talking-during-announcements smile at Sparrow and pointed to her seat.

Sparrow sat down. She scanned the name cards of

the other kids in her pod. Two boys and a girl. Paloma. Anton. Caleb. In the middle of their pod stood a dowel topped with a circle of blue construction paper. They were the blue pod.

The booming voice went on. *"I'm Principal Weiss, and I want to give a big Eastbrook welcome to all our new student learners!* Bienvenue. Bienvenidos. Ahlan wa sahlan. *And if you are a returning student learner, welcome back! Here at Eastbrook Elementary, we are proud to have students from all over the world! And now, from all of us to all of you, good morning!"*

There was a pause, and then a recording came on with kids' voices saying something—it must have been "good morning"—in other languages. Sparrow didn't like being new. She didn't like wondering who was going to be her friend instead of having one already. But she wasn't from a whole other country. Other kids were new here *and* from far away. That sounded hard.

"All right, fourth graders," said Mrs. Foxworthy when announcements were over, "now we're going to introduce ourselves. I'd like everyone to please share a fun fact about yourself."

They started on the other side of the room. Sparrow should have been listening. She should have been thinking of her fun fact. But all she could think about was Mrs. LaRose and the cats. Was Mrs. LaRose going to be on crutches? Or in a wheelchair? And what were the cats doing right now? Were they okay, alone all day?

"Hey," said the kid across from her, interrupting her thoughts.

It was the boy with the name card ANTON. He wore a T-shirt with a dog on it. It wasn't just a tiny picture of a tiny dog. The whole shirt was the face of a dog.

"Hey," he repeated, "Sparrow *Robin*son. Get it? That's, like, two birds in your name."

"I know," whispered Sparrow. "I get it."

"So who would win?" asked Anton. "Sparrow or robin?"

Sparrow gave a little shrug. "I don't know."

"Guess what?" asked the other girl in their pod, Paloma. "My name means 'pigeon' in Spanish. So we both have bird names!"

Sparrow instantly wanted two things. One, to be friends with Paloma. Two, a headband like Paloma's, with two kitty-cat ears on top.

"Okay, who would win *that*?" demanded Anton. "Sparrow or pigeon?"

"That's stupid," said Paloma, turning to Sparrow with a *Can you believe this kid?* look on her face. Her eyes were dark brown and her skin was the same golden brown as the cat ears resting on her head like a crown. "A sparrow and a pigeon wouldn't be in a fight."

Caleb, the other boy, said, "They might."

Caleb practically blended in with the cream-colored desk. He wore a white T-shirt, his face was pale, and his hair was blond. "What if they were both eating out of the same bird feeder, and there was only a single seed left? They might fight then."

But Anton seemed to have lost interest in birds, because he asked, "Who would win? Tiger or lion?"

"Blue pod!" said Mrs. Foxworthy. "Please be respectful listeners!"

Sparrow and the other kids in her pod stopped talking, and she went back to wondering how Mrs. LaRose and the cats were doing. Then suddenly it was the blue pod's turn.

Caleb went first. "I'm on level twelve of *EarthWatch Invasion*," he said. "When I finish that level, I'm going to be a Knight of EarthWatch."

Sparrow didn't think playing video games was much of a fun fact. But it was better than nothing, she supposed. Which was what she had.

Anton went next. "I'm saving up for a dog, and when I have enough, I'm going to get a really big one, like a Great Dane!"

Then Paloma went. "I had a cat," she said. "But we had to leave her when we moved here. She's still in the Dominican Republic."

Sparrow's turn.

"My fun fact," she said, stalling. Because she hadn't come up with anything yet, and now all she could think about was, where did Paloma get that kitty-cat headband and would she think Sparrow was copying her if she got one too?

"My fun fact," she said, "is I have seven cats."

⤜ 10 ⤝

Sparrow's legs were walking around the cafeteria, searching for a place to sit. But her head was busy asking, *Why? Why?* Why did she say she had seven cats? The words had just come out. And now she would have to admit it wasn't true. Or try to keep it a secret and hope nobody found out. One thing Sparrow knew, she was *not* good at keeping things inside. Everything she thought seemed to come flying out of her mouth. But why had something come flying out that wasn't true? And where was she supposed to sit, anyway? The cafeteria was so crowded. And noisy. And it smelled like pepperoni pizza.

One of the lunch ladies directing traffic stopped her. "Who's your teacher?"

"Mrs. Foxworthy."

Pointing, the lady said, "Foxworthy fourth graders over there."

At the Foxworthy fourth-grade table, Sparrow saw Paloma waving.

"I saved you a seat," called Paloma, pointing to the spot beside her.

It was the space in between what seemed to be the boys' end of the table and the girls' end. Sparrow didn't care. Boys'-side and girls'-side stuff was stupid. She slid onto the bench seat next to Paloma, with Anton and Caleb across from them. At either end of the table were kids whose names she didn't know yet.

"I can't believe you have seven cats," said Paloma. "What are their names?"

"Mrs. Moon, Midnight, Tux, Pierre, Paulette, Marmalade, and Kitty Gray." That was kind of like the truth, decided Sparrow, because those were their real names.

"How come your parents let you have seven cats?" asked Caleb. "Are they divorced or something?"

Sparrow bit into the pita pocket with hummus that her dad had packed for her lunch. She was wondering how to answer Caleb's question without lying when Paloma said, "You must have to clean the litter box every day." She pinched her nose with her fingers. *"Pee-yoo!"*

Anton and Caleb laughed and pinched their noses too.

"It sounds funny when I talk like this," said Anton, squeezing his nose.

"Me too," agreed Caleb. *"Pee-yoo."*

"Pee-yoo, pee-yoo, pee-yoo," they chanted.

"I miss my cat so much," said Paloma. "Except for that part. My mom used to clean the litter box, but then my dad started making me help him do it because my mom was pregnant with my little brother, and if you are going to have a baby, you are *not* allowed to be near cat poo."

"I know," said Sparrow, nodding. Which was not true. She didn't know anything about cat poo. Or babies.

"Sorry!" said Paloma. "I didn't mean to be a know-it-all."

"You're not!" said Sparrow, feeling bad. She was the one telling lies, and now Paloma was the one apologizing. This lie had just popped out, like the first one. It was like the lies were stuck together. Like when she touched a roasted marshmallow and her fingers got stuck together with melted goop. Sparrow liked marshmallows, but she did *not* like that sticky feeling.

Anton and Caleb were still holding their noses closed so everything they said sounded funny.

"Cat poo stinks," said Anton.

"It's stinky," agreed Caleb.

"Stinky, stinky, stinky," they chanted together.

"Come on," added Anton, tugging on Sparrow's sleeve. *"Talk like us."*

Sparrow and Paloma looked at each other. Were the boys being annoying? Or funny? Funny, they both decided, squeezing their noses between their fingertips at the exact same time.

"Hey," said Sparrow in a funny-sounding voice.

"Hey," echoed Paloma.

"Good," said Anton. *"Now say 'stinky, stinky, stinky' as fast as you can."*

"Stinky, stinky, stinky," said Paloma, giggling.

Talking in noses-squeezed-shut voices was funny. But Anton hogging Paloma was not. Sparrow leaned toward Paloma.

"Hey," she said. *"Want to know a secret?"*

"Totally," said Paloma.

"The secret," she said, stalling for time, *"is . . ."*

This was as bad as the fun fact! She didn't have a secret. But she did have something she hadn't told anybody yet, which was kind of like a secret.

"The secret is, I broke somebody's hip. And they had to go to the hospital—in an ambulance!"

"Whoa," said Anton, sounding impressed.

"No way!" said Paloma.

"Are you in trouble?" asked Caleb.

"No!" said Sparrow. *"It was by accident!"*

In a nose-squeezed-shut, funny-sounding voice she told them the story. The neighbor lady. The butterfly hatching from its chrysalis. The dancing and the lady falling over.

A bell rang. Lunch was over. The Foxworthy fourth graders began scrambling up from the table, and Sparrow and Paloma and Anton and Caleb had to stop squeezing their noses shut so they could clean up their trash.

"It's not really a secret," admitted Sparrow in a normal voice. "But nobody at school knows. Just you guys."

One little part of the story was actually, really a secret, though. The part she hadn't told them—how the lady with the broken hip was the person with seven cats. Not Sparrow.

"Hey," said Paloma as they headed out of the cafeteria. "Can I come over sometime? I take the bus, but if your mom calls my mom, and my mom calls the school, I can come tomorrow, okay?"

"Definitely," agreed Sparrow.

"And then I can see the cats!" added Paloma.

"Definitely," echoed Sparrow. "Yeah, for sure!"

She felt good. She felt great! It was the first day of school and she had made a friend. And tomorrow her friend might even come over.

There was just one problem.

Tomorrow her brand-new friend was going to find out she was a great big liar.

⤜ 11 ⤚

When Sparrow walked out of her first day at Eastbrook Elementary, she found both her mom and her dad waiting for her. She ran into her dad's hug, and for a second she held still, with his arms wrapped around her, until she started feeling squished. Then she ducked out and away.

"Wait, how come you're here?" she asked. "How come you're not at work?"

"It's your first day of school!" he said. "So I took the day off too. I didn't think it was fair for Mom to have all the fun."

The three of them began heading home. All along the sidewalk were other families going in the same direction, away from school, with parents pushing strollers and kids walking or rolling on scooters. High overhead, white clouds were drifting across a blue sky.

"So how'd it go?" asked her mom.

"I made a friend!"

"That didn't take long!" said her dad with a big smile. "That's great!"

"Mom, can she come over tomorrow? Can you call her mom?"

"Well, yes!" said her mom, sounding surprised. "Tomorrow, that could work! But next week's a different story. I still don't know where you'll be after school."

"Mom, I have to come home after school. I have to take care of the cats. I promised!"

"Sparrow, you promised to take care of the cats," said her dad. "You didn't promise to be with them from three thirty to four thirty, exactly."

"Daddy, stop!" said Sparrow. She hated when he used facts to argue.

"Stop what?" he asked.

"Stop . . . fact-fighting!"

Sparrow's mom laughed. "She's got you there, Dan. You do argue with facts. And I understand, Sparrow, this isn't about facts for you. It's about how you *feel*."

"*Mom,*" she groaned. She didn't want to argue about facts with her dad. Because he would always win that fight. And she didn't want to talk about feelings with her mom. Because that made her feel squished. "Why can't I just be home by myself? It's only one hour!"

"Someday you can," said her mom, "but not yet. Because accidents happen, right?"

This conversation felt like two against one. Which made Sparrow mad. "Don't you think I know that?" she shouted. "I'm the one who called 911, remember?"

"Take it easy, kiddo," said her dad. "We know you did."

"And we hear that you want to be able to stay home alone," added her mom, "but that is not going to happen right away. So let's put a pin in that idea, and we'll discuss it again in a few months."

As far as Sparrow could tell, her parents always wanted her to take it easy. They never wanted her to get upset. Or excited. Or what they called "carried away."

"Can we just go see the cats?" she asked.

"Good idea," said her mom.

They walked down Bridge Street and up Hartley Street, and when they reached the house, her dad said, "First things first. We have something to show you." He explained that Mrs. LaRose's side of the house would be kept locked now. He showed her where to find the key, hanging from a hook on their kitchen wall, and how to unlock Mrs. LaRose's door. Then together they all went inside.

Nothing had changed since Sparrow left that morning. There was the tall clock, ticking off the minutes.

There were the salt and pepper shakers (white cat for salt, black cat for pepper) on the lazy Susan. Even the cats were in their usual spots. Pierre and Paulette on the windowsill, between the geraniums. Midnight draped on top of the comfy chair. Marmalade gazing down from his perch on top of the refrigerator. And here came Mrs. Moon, padding over and asking to be petted. Sparrow knelt down and stroked the cat's soft white fur, and Mrs. Moon began purring. Sparrow loved that sound—a humming, thrumming sound as soft as the cat's fur.

Another noise sounded—the buzzing of a cell phone. Sparrow's mom pulled hers out of her pocket. "Perfect timing!" she said as she answered. "There's somebody here who would love to say hello. I'm going to put you on speaker." She set the phone on the table.

"Hello?" came a voice.

"Mrs. LaRose!" said Sparrow.

"Hi, everyone," came another voice. "This is Jenny."

When all the hellos were done Mrs. LaRose asked, "Sparrow, how is our butterfly? Did she fly away?"

Sparrow had been so busy with the cats and the first day of school, she had forgotten all about the butterfly. "I think so," she said. "It's gone."

"She has gone to Mexico for the winter. It's a long journey. And how are the cats?"

"Good," said Sparrow. "Listen to Mrs. Moon!" She took the phone and held it close to the cat, and everyone listened to the thrumming sound of her purring.

"Ah, she purrs!" said Mrs. LaRose. "Thank you! Now listen, Sparrow, I'll be home soon. And until then, you take care of the cats, *oui*?"

Oui was French for "yes."

"*Oui!*" said Sparrow, stroking Mrs. Moon's soft white fur.

"Mom," said the voice of Mrs. LaRose's daughter, Jenny. "Remember, you might need to go to rehab first. We don't know when you'll be back at the house."

Jenny LaRose was talking to her mom using the same voice Sparrow's parents used when they talked to her. The being-reasonable voice. Which was weird. Mrs. LaRose was the mom, so how come Jenny was trying to act like *she* was the one in charge? Sparrow always thought that when you got to be a grown-up, you were in charge of yourself.

"A few days," said Mrs. LaRose. "The doctor said a few days."

"But we don't really know," said Jenny. "Which is why I think the best thing is for me to take the cats somewhere."

Sparrow didn't like the sound of that. "Somewhere like *where*?" she asked.

"Like a shelter," said Jenny, "where people adopt cats."

"No!" said Sparrow and Mrs. LaRose in unison.

"Mom," said Jenny. "We've discussed this! It's going to happen sooner or later."

"But not yet . . . ," began Mrs. LaRose, and then they couldn't hear words anymore, just the muffled sound of voices, as if the other phone had been hidden under a pillow.

Sparrow's mom and dad traded a worried look, and her dad called out, "Hello?"

"Hello?" her mom echoed. "Hello?"

But nobody answered.

⚡ 12 ⚡

Sparrow and her mom and dad waited for somebody to answer. Waiting, Sparrow stroked Mrs. Moon's fur. So soft! It always made Sparrow feel better. Three times she ran her hand from the top of Mrs. Moon's head, along her back, to the tip of her tail.

Finally, Jenny LaRose came back on. "Sorry about that," she said. "That's a conversation for another day. Anyway, thank you so much for taking care of things there for—well, for now."

"Of *course*," said Sparrow's dad. "Whatever you need."

"Absolutely, we've got it covered," said her mom, and, wrapping up the call, she added, "Okay, keep us posted. Talk soon. Bye!" She tapped off the phone.

"She can't just give away the cats!" cried Sparrow. "They're not *hers*!"

"That's up to the two of them," said Sparrow's mom. "So let's not get carried away worrying about something that's not our business."

"Agreed," said Sparrow's dad. "Let's focus on right now. We can pick up more cat food when we go shopping, and Sparrow can keep feeding them."

"And washing the saucers!" Sparrow chimed in.

"What about the litter box?" asked Sparrow's mom. "That's a big job."

"Do not go near that litter box!" said her dad, holding up his hand like a stop sign.

Sparrow heard the alarm in her dad's voice. She saw his stop-sign hand. She remembered what Paloma had said, about moms and babies and cat poo.

"What," she said, "is Mom going to have a *baby*?"

Sparrow's mom and dad looked at each other. Looked at Sparrow. Looked back at each other. Then began laughing. Were they laughing at her? Because she was so stupid that she hadn't known?

Suddenly she felt the cat's soft head bump against her hand: *Pet me*. She hadn't realized she had stopped, and her hands were bunched tight. She unbunched them and began petting Mrs. Moon again, and the cat started up purring.

"I am," said her mom, smiling. "*We* are," she corrected herself. "Our family is having a baby. It will be all of ours."

That didn't make sense to Sparrow. It was like when people said, "I'm not laughing *at* you, I'm laughing *with* you." But if you weren't laughing, they couldn't be laughing with you. It wasn't their whole family having a baby. It was her mom.

"How come you didn't tell me?" she demanded.

"We haven't told anyone else," explained her mom. "And we didn't want to ask you to keep a secret. But how did you know about toxoplasmosis?"

"Paloma. She has a cat, and she has a little brother. And I can keep a secret!"

Sparrow's dad began explaining that the baby was the reason they had moved here. They needed more space. Also—more good news—this place wasn't just bigger. Soon it was going to be theirs. They were buying the house from Mrs. LaRose.

"But she can still live here, right? And keep her cats?"

"She can stay as long as she wants," said her dad. "That's part of the deal."

"And the cats can stay too, right?" pressed Sparrow.

But nobody answered her question. Her mom and dad both got up from their chairs and went in for a hug, each of them holding out an arm toward Sparrow. She got to her feet and joined the hug. They were so excited, and part of her wanted to be excited too. Instead all she could think about was whether Jenny LaRose was really going to get rid of all the cats. And all she felt—right in the middle of a squeezed-tight group hug—was left out.

"Squished," she said, and wriggled free.

⅄ 13 ⅄

The second day of school was a blur. Sparrow couldn't pay attention to anything Mrs. Foxworthy said. Because, one: Paloma was coming over today! Which was excellent. And, two: Mrs. LaRose's daughter wanted to do something horrible. Which was so unfair. And, three: her mom was going to have a baby. Which was—Sparrow had no idea what it was. But it was a long time away. And Paloma coming over was finally happening right *now*. The last bell rang, and Sparrow and Paloma swung their backpacks onto their shoulders and walked out together.

"Who would win?" asked Anton, right beside them. "Tarantula or scorpion?"

"I don't know," said Sparrow.

They passed a bulletin board with words in different

construction paper colors. WELCOME in yellow. BIENVENUE in green. BIENVENIDOS in orange. AHLAN WA SAHLAN in purple.

"Besides, would that ever happen?" asked Paloma. "In real life? Are they enemies?"

"Who cares?" asked Anton. "Okay, who would win? Killer whale or great white shark?"

They went past another board with a big yellow construction paper sun and the words RISE AND SHINE AT EASTBROOK ELEMENTARY.

"Um," said Sparrow. "I'm thinking . . ."

What she was thinking was they were almost at the big door that led outside, where they would be free from Anton and his questions.

"Come on," said Anton. "Killer whale or great white shark?"

They made it through the door. Outside it was *hot*. The kind of hot where nobody wanted to be in the sun. Sparrow spotted her mom standing with a bunch of other parents, under the shade of a tree.

"We gotta go," she said, heading for the tree.

"But just guess," he said, trooping along beside them.

"I can't," she said, and pointed. "There's my mom. I gotta go."

"Very funny," said Anton. "That's *my* mom."

"Hi, honey," called Sparrow's mom.

"Hey, sweetie," called a lady next to Sparrow's mom.

Right at the same time, Sparrow replied "Hi, Mom" to *her* mom and Anton replied "Hi, Mom" to *his* mom.

"Jinx!" said Paloma, and Sparrow and Anton looked at each other. Was this funny? wondered Sparrow. Or was this so *not* funny?

"Hi, Sparrow," said her mom. "And you must be Paloma! Nice to meet you."

Paloma gave a little wave.

"Sparrow, I've got great news!" said her mom. "I want you to meet Mrs. Randolph."

Sparrow recognized her. It was the same lady her mom had been talking to yesterday at drop-off, with the hot-pink sundress. In addition to wearing Sparrow's favorite color, Mrs. Randolph had what Sparrow thought was the perfect never-have-to-comb-your-hair hairstyle—short locs.

There were hellos all around, and then all five of them began walking in the same direction. As they walked, the moms told them the plan. Mrs. Randolph ran a day care in her house, with little ones during the day and some older kids in the afternoons. This week she had closed for Labor Day and the first couple of days of school, but starting next week she'd be back at work, and anytime Sparrow needed, she could walk home with Anton for the afternoon.

"Isn't that great?" asked Sparrow's mom. "And they're right on our street!"

"It is *so* great!" agreed Mrs. Randolph. "Anton really helps me out playing with the toddlers and all, but it'll be nice for him to have a friend his own age there. Imagine how happy I was when I saw you kids walking out together. Talk about divine intervention!"

"Absolutely," agreed Sparrow's mom.

By now they had passed the library and the church and the bakery and turned onto Hartley Street. In a little bit they came to the house with the ladybug flag hanging from the front porch.

"This is us," said Mrs. Randolph. "So we'll say good-bye."

"Wait—why don't you come over?" asked Sparrow's

mom. "Anton can play with the girls, and I've got some iced tea in the fridge."

"Iced tea does sound nice," said Anton's mom.

"*Mom*," said Sparrow. "Mom, Mom, *Mom!*" Which meant, *I have a playdate.*

Her mom put her hand on Sparrow's shoulder and gave a little squeeze. Which meant, *I know that. Change of plans. Don't be rude.*

Being rude was a big no-no in Sparrow's family. But Sparrow wasn't trying to be rude. She wasn't trying to hurt Anton's feelings. But if his feelings got hurt because she already had a playdate with Paloma, then too bad! That wasn't her fault! That seemed so obvious to her. How come it wasn't obvious to her mom?

"On second thought," said Mrs. Randolph, looking straight at Sparrow, "we don't want to butt in."

"But I want to see the cats!" said Anton.

"Anton," said his mom, "these girls don't need you pestering them about which creature would beat some other creature in some imaginary fight." She gave Sparrow a little wink. "Am I right?"

Sparrow's mom said, "Oh, come on. The girls will be fine."

For a minute they all stood on the street, in the hot sun, as the moms debated. Sparrow's mom seemed to care more about Anton's feelings than *her* feelings.

Just like Anton's mom seemed to care more about Sparrow's feelings than her own kid's. Which was weird. And confusing. And annoying.

Then Anton said, "Who would win? Your mom or my mom?"

Everybody laughed, which wasn't a solution but somehow seemed to settle things, because Paloma cried, "Let's race!" and all three of them took off running.

↘ 14 ↙

"**C**ome on," Sparrow said, unlocking the door to Mrs. LaRose's unit and leading Paloma and Anton inside. With the door still open wide, they could hear the moms chatting as they settled into lawn chairs on the porch. Sparrow closed the door behind them. Now all they heard was the ticking of the tall clock at the end of the hallway.

In the kitchen, Mrs. Moon rushed over and began slinking in figure eights around Sparrow's ankles. Sparrow plunked herself down on the kitchen floor and began patting the cat's soft white fur. "This is Mrs. Moon."

The two brown tabbies were perched on the window-sill, between the pots of geraniums. One of them jumped down—his tail brushing the geraniums, making the room smell like lemons—and came over to be patted. "This is Pierre," she said. The other tabby stayed put, licking her paws. "That's Paulette."

She pointed to the orange tabby on top of the fridge. "That's Marmalade."

The black cat with a white throat padded into the kitchen. "That's Tuxedo, because of his white collar. The all-black one is Midnight," she added, pointing to the comfy chair.

"This is six cats," said Paloma. "You said seven."

"Kitty Gray is outside. She only shows up when it's time to eat."

"Okay, let's play veterinarian," said Paloma. "I'll be the vet and you bring your cats to me because they're sick."

"How come you get to be the vet?" asked Anton.

"Because it's my idea," said Paloma.

"Okay, whatever," said Anton, patting Pierre, "you're the vet. And I'm bringing in my cat because she's going to have kittens."

"Pierre is a boy cat," said Sparrow. "He can't have kittens."

"Says you," said Anton. "You're not the boss of my cat."

"Yes, she is!" said Paloma. "They're *her* cats, remember?"

Sparrow jumped in to join the Sparrow-and-Paloma team. "Yeah, they're *my* cats," she pushed back, without thinking what she was doing. Doubling down on her lie.

"Okay, okay," said Anton, pivoting. "Then who's a girl cat?"

"Mrs. Moon," said Sparrow. "She could have kittens."

"Or puppies!" said Anton. "What if she had puppies instead of kittens?"

"Anton," groaned Paloma, "that's not the game!"

Sparrow sided with Paloma. "We're not playing that, Anton."

Paloma was looking all around. "What's that?" she asked, pointing to the big black telephone on the wall.

"It's a phone," said Sparrow. "It's old fashioned, but it works."

Just then the clock sounded the hour. *Gong. Gong. Gong. Gong.*

"What was *that*?" asked Paloma.

"The clock," said Sparrow. "Four gongs means it's four o'clock. When it goes five times, that's when I feed them."

"How come?" asked Anton.

"That's when . . . ," began Sparrow. She almost said, *That's when Mrs. LaRose always feeds them*, but caught herself. "That's their suppertime."

"Your house is like a museum or something," said Paloma.

"Totally," agreed Anton. "We went to this place once where everyone was dressed up like they lived in olden times. It's like that."

"It's like you don't really *live* here," added Paloma. "You know?"

"Want a Popsicle?" asked Sparrow, scrambling to her feet.

She had no idea if there were any Popsicles in Mrs. LaRose's freezer. So right then she made a deal with herself. She wasn't going to tell *another* lie. If there were no Popsicles, and if they had to go next door to find the Popsicles in her own fridge, she would fess up.

She opened the freezer door. Popsicles! Not time to confess now, she figured as she handed out Popsicles.

"Where's your room?" asked Paloma. "Can we play there?"

Licking a lemon Popsicle covered with ice fuzz, Sparrow answered, "Um, my mom doesn't let me eat food upstairs."

That wasn't the real reason not to show them her room. The real reason was that her bedroom wasn't up the stairs at the end of the hall. It was next door. They would have to go out Mrs. LaRose's front door and in Sparrow's family's front door to get there. But it wasn't totally a lie, either, because her mom really didn't let her eat food upstairs.

And that was how the rest of the afternoon went. In order to avoid telling Paloma and Anton the truth, she had to say a bunch of things that weren't exactly lies but felt like lies because they weren't the whole story. She managed to do that for the next hour, until the clock sounded five. Then they fed the cats, and then Sparrow's mom hollered for them to come outside because Paloma's mom was here to pick her up.

Outside, the three moms were standing under the shade of a big tree. In the yard next door a sprinkler was going back and forth, throwing drops of water across the hot blue sky.

"Thank you for having her over," said Paloma's mom. "Honey, come say *gracias*."

"Thanks, Mrs. Robinson," said Paloma to Sparrow's mom, and to Sparrow she said, "You're going to have the best report of anybody."

"What report?" asked Mrs. Randolph. "Anton, do you have a report due?"

"Sort of," said Anton. "We're supposed to take turns telling the class more about our fun fact. A couple kids will go every day."

"We're supposed to try and paint a picture with words," explained Paloma.

Sparrow's mom asked her, "What was your fact, sweetie?"

Paloma answered for Sparrow, "Having seven cats!"

"Really?" asked Sparrow's mom, turning to Sparrow with a strange look on her face. The look that said, *Tell me I didn't just hear that you told a great big fat lie.*

↘ 15 ↙

Sparrow waited for her mom to call her out.
But her mom didn't say anything as Paloma and her
mom got in their car and drove off. Then right away
Anton's mom started talking.

"We better get going too. Oh, and I almost forgot—
if you're looking for a church, why don't you come
with us to First Parish this Sunday? It's right around
the corner on Bridge Street. Anton's going to be in the
children's choir, aren't you, Anton?" She kept talking
without waiting for Anton to answer. "And I know the
choir director would love to have you join us," she said
to Sparrow.

"We're not really churchgoers," said her mom. "At
least, we haven't been. But maybe—I don't know. I'll
think about it."

"Great!" said Mrs. Randolph. "You have a think, and I'm going to ask again, because that's how I am. Now, when do you expect Mrs. LaRose back? Because I'll be sure to send a casserole. She is such a sweet lady. You know, she goes to First Parish too!"

"Who's Mrs. LaRose?" asked Anton.

"You know her," said his mom. "She's the lady at church with all the hats! This is where she lives."

"The hat lady lives *here*?" asked Anton. "I thought this was *your* house," he said to Sparrow.

Next door, water droplets from the neighbor's sprinkler swept through the sky. They went one way, raining down on the neighbor's lawn. Then they went the other way, landing on the driveway.

Sparrow was figuring that her mom would say something *now*. But her mom still wasn't saying anything. She wasn't calling Sparrow out. But she wasn't rescuing her either. Sparrow was on her own.

"It is," said Sparrow. "We live in one half and Mrs. LaRose lives in the other."

Anton thought about that for a second, then demanded, "What about the cats? You said they were yours!"

It was so quiet, Sparrow could hear the sound of water droplets splattering the driveway. *Splat, splat, splat.*

"They're not mine," she admitted. "They're Mrs. LaRose's."

"What?" cried Anton. "You said they were yours! You are *so busted.*"

"All right, Anton, that's enough," said Mrs. Randolph. "It's time to go. Thank you so much for the iced tea and the company, Susan," she added, and she took Anton by the hand and headed down Hartley Street.

Sparrow and her mom stood in the shade, waving goodbye. Then, finally, they were all alone.

"Wow," said her mom. "Just—wow. That was a whopper. What got into you?"

"I don't know," said Sparrow, shrugging. "It just came out!"

"When? How?"

"When we had to share a fun fact, on the first day. And I couldn't think of anything."

"Well," said her mom, shaking her head. "You'll have to come clean, you know."

"I *know*," said Sparrow. She knew her mom would say that. Her mom wanted everything to be like clean teeth. Nice clean brushed teeth with no cavities. Nice clean words with no lies in them. "You don't have to tell me that."

"Don't get snippy with me," said her mom. "Now, do you want to call Paloma so you can get it over with?"

Why did grown-ups ask if you wanted to do something that they knew you didn't want to do *at all*? Of course she didn't want to call Paloma!

"No," she said. "I'll do it at school."

"Promise?" asked her mom. "First thing Monday morning?"

"Yes," she answered as the sprinkler went *splat, splat, splat*. "Promise."

↘ 16 ↙

Sunday morning Sparrow had gone to feed the cats, and Mrs. Moon had followed her back, slinking along at her heels. Standing outside on the porch, Sparrow opened the front door and popped her head in. "Hey, Mom, can Mrs. Moon come in? She's, like, attaching herself to my legs."

"Honey, the cats belong next door or outside," said her mom from her seat at the kitchen table. "I don't want them over here. Cats shed, and I'm the one who has to vacuum."

"Mom, just for a little bit? Not to *stay*. Just for *right now*."

Her mom took a sip of coffee, then took a look at her dad. Her dad looked back at her mom. They were having one of those conversations that Sparrow couldn't *hear* but she could *see*.

Mom: *We said no cats allowed over here.*

Dad: *We did.*

Mom: *Positive parenting means being consistent.*

Dad: *It does. But . . .*

But there was something else going on. Sparrow could *feel* it. Something secret.

"All right," her mom finally said. "But don't get used to this, okay?"

"Thank you!" said Sparrow, coming in with Mrs. Moon. "Thank you, thank you, thank you. *French toast!*" she added, seeing the food on the kitchen table. "French toast, French toast, French toast!" She plunked herself down in her seat and reached for the maple syrup. Mrs. Moon jumped into her lap, circled a couple of times, getting comfortable, then settled down, purring.

"That's a happy cat," observed her dad.

Sparrow was too busy chewing to answer, so she just nodded.

"After you finish," said her mom, "I want you to go upstairs and put on a sundress."

"How come?"

"Because I said so," said her mother.

Sparrow's mom wasn't usually a "Because I said so" kind of mom. Usually she gave a reason, like "No cats because they shed and I'm the one who has to vacuum."

"That's not a reason," objected Sparrow. "I just want to know *why*."

"Because we're going to church," said her mother.

"Church?" echoed Sparrow. "We never go to church."

"Not never," corrected her dad. "Rarely. We rarely go to church."

"Okay, whatever! We *hardly ever* go to church. Why are we going now?"

All she could remember from the couple of times they'd gone—once at Christmas and once at Easter—was having to sit still, and be quiet, for what felt like forever. She hated sitting still and being quiet. Was this the secret behind her parents' back-and-forth looks? *Let's be nice to Sparrow now because we're just about to spring something on her that she won't like?*

"Mrs. Randolph said it's a really nice neighborhood church," said her mom. "I think it will be a good way to feel like part of the community. Get to know some more people around here."

Sparrow already knew plenty of people from school. "Do I have to go?"

"Yes," said her mom and dad in unison.

Half an hour later Sparrow had changed into a sundress and put Mrs. Moon back in Mrs. LaRose's unit. Outside, the day was getting hotter. The next-door neighbor's sprinkler was on again, flinging drops of water back and forth. Her parents were standing in the shade of the big tree.

Her mom gave her dad a kiss. "See you later," she said.

"Dad's not coming?" cried Sparrow. "That's not fair! Why can't I stay home with him?"

"Because you're coming with me," said her mom.

Sparrow thought that was another not-really-a-reason reason. And she thought she knew the real reason. Her mom was trying to fix her. As usual. "Is this because I lied about the cats?"

"No!" said her mom. "Listen, Little Bird. Going to church isn't a punishment. Of course I want you to tell the truth. But I know there are—well, there are different kinds of lies. That was a wishful-thinking kind of lie. You said something you wished was true. You weren't trying to hurt anyone."

"That was a pretty big wish," said her dad. "You don't really want seven cats, do you?"

"No," said Sparrow. "But I wish we could have one cat."

Sparrow's mom didn't respond to that. "Listen, I want you to come because I want all of us to go together, as a family. And maybe you can do children's choir. That would be great for you!"

Sparrow didn't bother responding to that. "If we're going together, how come Daddy doesn't have to come?"

"I'll come next time," he said. "But today I need to get started on something. I'm building a ramp for when Mrs. LaRose comes home."

"*When?*" cried Sparrow. "When is she coming home?"

"Soon," said her dad.

"Let's get moving," said her mom. "Or we'll be late."

Sparrow didn't need to be told to get moving. She took off, zooming in a circle around her parents. But that circle wasn't big enough for how she felt. Mrs. LaRose was coming home! They would eat cookies, drink lemonade, and pet the cats. And Mrs. LaRose wouldn't try to fix anything about her. Sparrow zoomed in a bigger circle around the lawn. Still not big enough.

She was heading around again just as the neighbor's sprinkler rose high in the sky. Now the sprinkler was sweeping back down. Sparrow saw that she could time it just right. She sped up. Changed course.

Her mom saw what was coming too. "Sparrow," she warned, "don't even think about it."

Sparrow wasn't thinking. She was racing. Toward the exact. Right. Spot.

"Sparrow," her mom called again. "Sparrow! *Sparrow!*"

Too late. Sparrow was dancing a little sprinkler dance of joy.

⚘ 17 ⚘

That night Sparrow lay in bed. After an afternoon thunderstorm, the hot-hot weather had left. It was still warm enough for open windows, but not hot enough to need a fan. In the quiet she could hear crickets chirping.

Even though school had started last week, it felt like the weather was just catching up, changing from "summer vacation" to "back-to-school autumn." And Sparrow was feeling back-to-school nervous about tomorrow. Last week her mom had stayed home and made pancakes for breakfast, and school was just getting-to-know-you stuff. This week her mom was going back to work, and school would start for real. And she had to tell Paloma the truth.

Not just Paloma. Sometime—maybe tomorrow—

Mrs. Foxworthy would ask her to expand on her fun fact. Then she'd have to tell the whole class that she didn't have seven cats. She didn't have *any* cats.

It took Sparrow a long time to fall asleep, and the next morning she woke to the sound of her dad calling up the stairs, "Sparrow, time to get ready for school! I'll be outside, working on the ramp. Call me if you need anything, okay?"

Sparrow scrambled to get ready. Get dressed. Feed the cats. Put lunch bag into backpack.

Outside, Hartley Street felt different. The air felt cooler, and the next-door neighbor wasn't running the sprinkler anymore. In Sparrow's front yard a few bright orange leaves hung from the big maple tree, like they were waving goodbye to summer.

But the biggest change was the beginnings of the long wooden ramp running up and over the porch steps. Whenever Mrs. LaRose got here, she could get into the house.

"Okey-doke," said her dad. "You know the plan, right?"

"I *know*," said Sparrow. "Mom told me a hundred times. After school walk with Anton to his house, and then Mom will call Mrs. Randolph when she gets home."

"Good," said her dad. "And you're sure you want to walk *to* school by yourself? Because I'm happy to go with you, if you want. But no big deal if you don't."

Walking to school was the one thing she was *not* worried about. "Dad, I'm not a baby. I'm in fourth grade."

"Not a baby," he said, giving her a quick hug. "Got it."

She slipped on her backpack and set off down Hartley Street. At the end of the street, she turned left onto Bridge Street. She walked past the yummy smell of cinnamon coming out of the bakery. It made her stomach growl, and she suddenly couldn't remember eating breakfast. She had fed the cats but not herself.

Just past the bakery was the church and the place where she crossed the street. Sparrow pushed the crosswalk button and waited for the walking-person light to flash.

Church yesterday had been long and boring. Her mom said next week would be more fun because that's when Sunday school started up. Sparrow wasn't sure she liked the sound of that—going to school all week and then having to go on Sunday, too. But maybe it would be better than sitting through the whole service. The only parts she had liked were the singing and the way the sun shone through the big stained-glass windows, making beams of red and blue and yellow light.

The crosswalk light began flashing, and Sparrow darted across the street.

The closer she got to school, the more nervous she felt about facing Paloma. As she walked into Eastbrook Elementary, her stomach felt as fluttery as if she were a kindergartner on her first day.

In the hallway outside their classroom, she spotted Paloma, along with a couple of other kids, getting things from their lockers—Caleb, from their pod, and Anna, a girl who sat at the yellow pod.

"Hey," said Paloma. "That was so much fun!"

"I know!" agreed Sparrow.

"What was so much fun?" asked Anna.

Paloma pushed her locker closed with a click. "I went over to Sparrow's and played with her cats," she boasted. "She has seven!"

"No fair!" said Caleb. "I like cats. Can I come over sometime?"

"Me too," said Paloma. "I mean, can I come over again?"

"Um, I doubt it," said Sparrow. "I have to go to after-care starting this week. Sorry," she added as the bell rang, and everybody trooped into the classroom.

That wasn't what she was supposed to say! But it felt like the words she was supposed to say were stuck inside her, making the flutters in her stomach worse and worse. By the time Mrs. Foxworthy asked for somebody to share more about their fun fact, and Paloma raised her hand, Sparrow's stomach felt like the time her family had gone whale-watching on a big boat. Sort of empty and growly. Sort of pukey.

Paloma got up and stood in front of the whiteboard. "My fun fact was that I'm from the DR and my cat is still there, which isn't really fun, but it's a fact. She lives there with my *tía* Eva. My cat's name is Nina, and she's all black except for her white paws."

Mrs. Foxworthy slid her red eyeglasses to the top of her head. "Can you tell us a story about your cat?" she asked. "And remember, storytellers use *vivid details*."

"Once Nina caught a mouse," said Paloma, "and she brought it to my mom. And the mouse was, like, *dead*. And my mom screamed a bad word! And my little brother was learning to talk, and he said it over and over, like, '*Bad-word, bad-word, bad-word.*' So my dad started calling the cat by that word, like, 'There's the *bad-word* cat,' which made my mom really mad."

Everybody laughed, and Mrs. Foxworthy raised her hand in the air, signaling for silence. "Okay," she finally said when they were quiet. "Does anyone have a question or a comment?"

"What was the bad word?" shouted Orion from the red pod.

"Paloma will *not* be answering that question," said Mrs. Foxworthy, shaking her head, so that the red glasses perched atop her head pointed back and forth too, as if they were saying, *No, no, no.* "Does anyone else have an *appropriate* question?"

Anna from the yellow pod raised her hand. "Are you going to get another cat?"

"I hope so," said Paloma. "I'm trying to talk my mom into it."

"Thank you, Paloma," said Mrs. Foxworthy, and Sparrow sensed her scanning the room for somebody to give the next report. Sparrow looked down so Mrs. Foxworthy couldn't make eye contact. *Don't call on me,* she thought, *don't call on me, don't call on me.* She wondered if that counted as a prayer. In church there had been a time for prayers. But they were all for big things, like that the planet would be healthy. She wondered if you were allowed to pray for something as small as not wanting the teacher to call your name.

"Sparrow!" said Mrs. Foxworthy. "Are you ready to expand on your fun fact?"

Sparrow got up and trudged to the talking spot in front of the whiteboard. "Um," she began, then stopped. Her stomach growled. "I have a stomachache."

Caleb's hand shot up in the air. "I have a question! Do you think you're going to barf?"

Everybody began to laugh, and kids were shouting things like "Eww!" and "Gross!"

"I have a question too!" shouted Anton. "You don't *really* have seven cats, do you?"

Now Sparrow didn't feel like she was in a boat, on *top* of the water. She felt like the time she was at the beach and a big wave crashed on her, sucking her *under* the water. There was a roaring in her ears. She couldn't breathe. Finally she drew a breath.

"Not exactly," she said. "I'm taking care of seven cats. But they're not mine."

A shocked silence fell over the room, so that everyone heard Paloma loud and clear. "You mean you, like, *tricked* me?" she asked. Then she threw Sparrow a single look of disgust and swiveled in her seat so Sparrow couldn't see her face anymore. All she could see was the back of Paloma's head, and the back of the kitty-cat ears on her headband.

⤝ 18 ⤞

"**W**here does it hurt?" asked Mrs. Pendleton, the school nurse.

Sparrow put her hand on her belly. "Here," she said, making a little moaning noise as she looked around. On the walls of the nurse's office hung posters for things like GERMS—BAD! and HANDWASHING—GOOD!

"Hmm," said Mrs. Pendleton. "Let's take your temperature." She held a thermometer to Sparrow's forehead. When it beeped, she studied it for a second, then pronounced, "Normal. How's that tummy?"

"It hurts," said Sparrow. Which was true. And when she thought about going back to class and facing Mrs. Foxworthy—nice Mrs. Foxworthy, who had changed her name card to Sparrow, and who had just let her come to the school nurse—it hurt more. And when she thought about facing Paloma, it hurt even more. "Ow," she said. This time with a groan.

Half an hour later her dad arrived, and halfway home, he pulled the car into a parking spot on Bridge Street. "I'll let work know I'm going to be late, so I can stay with you until mom gets home. And in the meantime, how would your stomach feel about a cinnamon roll?"

"Good!" said Sparrow. "I'm starving!"

"We both forgot your breakfast today, didn't we?" he asked as they sat down at one of the little tables on the sidewalk. "That's my bad. I was so busy working on the ramp, I totally spaced!"

"That's okay," she said as she bit into a soft, sweet roll. Sparrow liked this feeling. Sitting at one of the tiny round tables in front of the bakery. On one side of them were window boxes with flowers, and behind the windows, trays of rolls and muffins. On the other side was the sidewalk, where people were walking by. A woman hurried past with a little black-and-white dog. Then came a man pushing a baby stroller, and another guy talking on his phone. It was funny how everybody had something to hold in their hands. A phone or a dog's leash or a bag from the bakery.

Her dad sipped his coffee. "I used to get stomachaches in September too," he said.

"You did? How come?"

"Homework," he said. "I never did it."

"What?" cried Sparrow, almost choking on the bite in her mouth. *Her dad hadn't done his homework?* She tried to match the fact-correcting dad she knew with the idea of a dad who didn't do his homework when he was a kid. Nope. It made no sense. Nobody would believe it. A little scared of the answer, she asked, "Does Mom know?"

Her dad burst out laughing. "Yes, she knows," he said. "It's not a secret."

"But I didn't know," objected Sparrow.

"That's not the same thing," said her dad, brushing his mustache to wipe away any cinnamon roll crumbs. "I wasn't keeping it from you. It just hadn't come up yet. There's a lot you don't know about me. All the things that happened before you were born, or when you were too little to remember. Know what I mean?"

"I guess," said Sparrow, untwirling another bit from her roll. It was weird to think about her parents before she knew them. It made her head feel like it was turning in a spiral, like the cinnamon rolls. And maybe her dad not doing his homework didn't count as a secret, but the other things did. The fact that they were buying Mrs. LaRose's house. And the baby. That had definitely been a secret.

"So," asked her dad, "was this a didn't-do-your-homework stomachache?"

"No," she said with a shrug. "Not really."

"What does 'not really' mean?"

"It means Anton *told*!"

"Told what?"

"He told everybody I don't have seven cats. He just blabbed it out, before I had a chance! And now everybody's mad at me. Paloma probably hates me."

"I get it," said her dad. "It's a need-to-make-up-with-your-friend stomachache."

A woman walking along stopped at their table. Her hands were jammed into the pockets of her jean jacket, and her hair was pulled back into a tight ponytail.

"Excuse me," she said. "Can you help me out? I need money for the bus—I'm trying to get home." She sounded like she might cry.

Sparrow's dad took out his wallet and looked inside. "I'm sorry," he said. "I don't have any cash on me."

"I do!" said Sparrow. She unzipped the backpack at her feet and scrounged around inside it. Pencil box, spiral notebook . . . where was it? There, at the bottom: the little coin purse with five dollar bills her mom had put there for emergencies. She held them out in her hand.

"Wow," said the jean-jacket lady. But she didn't reach for the money right away. With her hands jammed in her pockets, she was looking at Sparrow's dad, having one of those grown-up conversations without words.

Jean-jacket lady: *Okay to take your kid's money?*

Sparrow's dad, with a nod: *Yes. Okay.*

"Thanks," she said, taking the crumpled bills. "That's wicked nice." She headed off down Bridge Street, toward the center of town.

"Was that enough?" Sparrow asked her dad. "For a bus ticket to get her home?"

"It depends. If she lives around here, yes. But not for a longer trip."

"We should have asked her how much she needed," said Sparrow.

"Well, you gave her everything you had. That was really generous of you. You're a good kid, Sparrow."

"But what if it's not enough? Daddy, I can still see her! Let's go catch up with her!"

"And then what?"

"We can ask her where *home* is and then go to the bank machine and take out the right amount of money!"

"Sparrow, honey, you're getting carried away."

"But I'm all done! Let's go!" She stood up so quickly, her chair toppled over behind her. The chair fell against another table, where somebody had left an empty coffee cup, and the cup toppled over too and fell to the ground. And broke.

"Sparrow!"

"I'm sorry!" she said, kneeling down to pick up the pieces.

"Stop!" said her dad,

holding on to her arm. "The last thing we need is you getting cut. Just—let me."

Sparrow stood back, watching her dad pick up the shards of the broken cup with a paper napkin. Their nice time at the bakery felt wrecked. And her dad wouldn't even let her help. It didn't seem fair to be mad at her for breaking a cup and mad at her for having to clean it up, too. At least she could pick up the chair. She set it on its legs.

Finally her dad finished cleaning up. "Daddy, can we go now? Can we look for her?"

"Sparrow, listen," said her dad. His face looked the way it did when he was playing word games on his phone. Like he was searching for words. "Helping people is important. That's why your mom and I give money to a couple of charities. But I can't always solve the problem of every person I meet on the street. You'll understand when you're older," he added. "Now let's go home."

She doubted it. She didn't think she would ever understand some things grown-ups did. Or, actually, the things they *didn't* do. They didn't buy bus tickets for people who needed them. They didn't run through sprinklers. They didn't get carried away about anything! They just plodded along.

She got into the car and buckled her seat belt, hoping she wasn't ever going to be a plodding-along grown-up when she grew up.

⤐ 19 ⤐

"Soon," Sparrow's dad had said. Mrs. LaRose was coming home soon. How come grown-ups could say things that weren't true *at all*, but it wasn't called a lie?

"Soon" would have been the same day he said it—Sunday, when he hadn't gone to church with Sparrow and her mom. Or the next day—Monday, when Anton had told the class that she was a big liar. But Mrs. LaRose hadn't come home Sunday or Monday. And she didn't come home the whole rest of the week. Tuesday or Wednesday or Thursday or Friday. The longest week of Sparrow's life.

School was the worst part of the day. Paloma wasn't speaking to her. She said things sometimes, but her words came out all cold and mean. Like when she pointed to the spot next to her in the cafeteria and said, "Somebody's sitting there." Or when she said, during recess, "I'm playing with Anna today. Sorry." Not sounding sorry at all.

Going to Anton's after school was the second-worst part of the day. Sparrow wanted to not talk to him, the same way Paloma wasn't talking to her. Because she was mad at him for Paloma being mad at her. But Anton either didn't care or didn't even notice. He just kept talking. Did she want to draw? Did she want to play LEGOs? Did she want to make dry-bean-and-paper-plate noisemakers and lead the little kids in a parade?

She usually just ended up playing with him until her mom called and she could go home to feed the cats. That was the best part of the day. By now she knew all their habits by heart. Where they liked to sit. How they liked to be patted.

Pierre and Paulette, the brown tabbies, liked the windowsill. When Sparrow came in, Pierre would jump down, brushing the geraniums and making the kitchen smell like lemons, and come say hello. Paulette stayed where she was, licking her white paws.

All-black Midnight thought he owned the comfy chair. He didn't budge from there, except for mealtimes. He liked tummy rubs.

She didn't know where black-and-white Tuxedo spent most of his time. But whenever she got there, he ambled into the kitchen from wherever he had been. He liked to be patted under his white throat and chin, as if he were saying, *See how fancy I am in my black suit and white shirt?*

Marmalade almost always perched on top of the fridge, like he was king of the castle. But sometimes he leapt down—fridge to counter, counter to floor—and came over for a pat. Then he would walk back and forth under her hand, from his orange head to the tip of his orange tail. Then turn around. Do it again.

Kitty Gray only showed up to eat, when she came to the door and meowed to be let in. She was the only *Don't pat me* cat.

And Mrs. Moon's favorite spot was wherever Sparrow was. She stuck close, slinking around Sparrow's ankles in figure eights if Sparrow was standing up. Settling in her lap when Sparrow sat down.

On Friday, after she got home from Anton's, Sparrow sprinted up the newly finished ramp. She gave her mom a quick hug, grabbed the key to Mrs. LaRose's, and ran next door. She fed the cats, and then—*finally*—she sat down in the comfy chair with her legs tucked up underneath her. Mrs. Moon jumped into her lap and circled a few times, then settled down, purring.

It had been a long week. Paloma was still giving her the silent treatment. Saying words but not really talking to her: "No cutting in line." "Mrs. Foxworthy says to

hand in our papers." "Sorry, I already have a partner." It was funny how silences could be so different. Paloma's silence was a mean silence. But the silence right now, in Mrs. LaRose's kitchen, was a nice silence. Softly ticking clock. Humming refrigerator. Purring cat. And nothing else. She closed her eyes.

She woke to somebody calling, "I'm home!"

⚡ 20 ⚡

"**I**'m home!" came the voice again, and Mrs. LaRose came trundling in, pushing a walker in front of her.

Sparrow and the cat both jumped. Mrs. Moon jumped *down* from Sparrow's lap, and Sparrow jumped *up* to say hi.

But a lady quickly stepped forward, holding her hand in the air like a stop sign. "Easy!" she said. "Safety first, right? One broken hip is enough. No offense," she added, changing her stop-right-there hand to a side-to-side wave. "You must be Sparrow. I'm Jenny."

"Hi," said Sparrow.

Jenny was a funny mixture of young-looking and old-looking. She had all-white hair, like Mrs. LaRose, but she wore it long and loose, not up in a bun or a braid. And she wore a black T-shirt, blue jeans, and sandals.

"Mom," said Jenny as she pulled one of the wooden chairs out from the table, "how about you sit *here*? And Sparrow will sit back down in *that* chair. That way everybody's safe, right?"

From their chairs, Sparrow and Mrs. LaRose both nodded. Yes. Right. Safe.

"Ma'am?" came a voice from the hallway. "Where do you want this?"

Two guys were bringing in a hospital bed so Mrs. LaRose could sleep on the ground floor. Jenny went to oversee them, and Sparrow and Mrs. LaRose were left alone in the kitchen with the cats. They looked at each other and giggled.

"It's good to be home," said Mrs. LaRose as the cats began leaving their spots and coming toward her. Marmalade jumped from atop the fridge, down to the kitchen counter, and down to the floor on his way over. Pierre leapt off the windowsill and onto her lap. Tux appeared from wherever he'd been and sat by her ankles.

Meanwhile, Mrs. Moon had clambered back onto Sparrow's lap.

"You have a new friend," said Mrs. LaRose.

"Do you want to hold her?" asked Sparrow.

"No, my hands are full," said Mrs. LaRose, stroking Pierre. "And it's good she made friends with you. She looks healthy—maybe a little plumper. Has she been stealing food from another kitty?"

"No!" said Sparrow. "They each got one can!"

"Good," said Mrs. LaRose. "And it's good she looks bigger. When she came here, she was very thin."

"Came here when?"

"About a month ago, just before you and your family arrived."

"I didn't know that!"

That was funny. Not funny ha-ha, but funny strange. It was strange to think that Mrs. Moon was almost as new here as Sparrow herself! Everything in Mrs. LaRose's house seemed like it had always been here. The clock. The phone. The cats.

She wondered what Mrs. Moon's name had been before. What if Mrs. Moon had another home somewhere, where people were really sad that she was gone? And what if Mrs. Moon really wanted to go there, like the lady in the jean jacket? On the other hand, what if Mrs. Moon liked it better here? Maybe her old owners hadn't fed her enough. It was weird to think of the cat having a whole other life before coming here. It was like Sparrow trying to imagine her dad in elementary school.

"Yes, it's true," said Mrs. LaRose. "She appeared one day. I didn't see any signs for a lost cat that looked like her, and I thought, *What is one more cat?*"

"Seven!" said Sparrow. "One more cat is seven! That's how many cats you have!"

"Now you know. Because you took care of them. Thank you, Sparrow."

Sparrow stroked Mrs. Moon's soft white fur. She wouldn't have been taking care of the cats if Mrs. LaRose hadn't broken her hip. And Mrs. LaRose wouldn't have broken her hip if she hadn't been taking care of Sparrow. No matter how she thought about it, it kept circling back to *her*. Sparrow being Sparrow.

"I'm sorry," she said. "Really, *really* sorry."

Mrs. LaRose said something that sounded like "Say lah vee," then added, "You know what this means?"

Sparrow shook her head.

"Get me paper and pen. I will show you."

Sparrow lifted Mrs. Moon off her lap—she *did* feel a little heavy—and got paper and a pen for Mrs. LaRose, who wrote down the words *C'est la vie*.

"It means 'That's life,'" said Mrs. LaRose. "Accidents happen. That's life. *C'est la vie, oui?*"

Sparrow already knew that one. *Oui*—which you said like the word "we"—meant "yes." "Okay, *oui*," she echoed, and tried the new words. *"C'est la vie."*

"Good!" said Mrs. LaRose as Sparrow's mom and Mrs. LaRose's daughter came into the kitchen.

"It's great to see you, Mrs. LaRose!" said Sparrow's mom. "We're so glad to have you back home. Sparrow, time to go, honey. And, Jenny, will you let us know how we can help? Can we pick up groceries? Or maybe take your mom to church on Sunday?"

"Let's see how she's feeling," said Jenny. "If she's up to it."

"She's right here," said Mrs. LaRose, "and she would love to go to church on Sunday. And next week," she added to Sparrow, "we'll have our afternoons with the cats again, *oui*?"

"Okay," said Sparrow. "I mean, *oui*!"

"Mom, wait," said Jenny. "We don't know what you'll be doing in the afternoon. The physical therapist might be coming then. And you need to focus on getting better. Not on Sparrow. No offense," she added, glancing at Sparrow's mom. "And not on all these cats, either, which are the biggest tripping hazard I ever saw."

Sparrow thought Jenny wouldn't have to spend so much time saying "no offense" if she didn't say so many kind-of-mean things.

"No, I totally understand," said Sparrow's mom. "Sparrow's been going to Mrs. Randolph's for aftercare this week. She can keep going there."

"No, no, no," said Mrs. LaRose. "I want to do this!"

It was Sparrow's mom and Mrs. LaRose's daughter against Mrs. LaRose and Sparrow. The plodding-along grown-ups against the cat-loving butterfly dancers.

Who would win?

⚡ 21 ⚡

"**W**elcome!" said the Sunday school lady. "I'm Miss Cathy, and this is my helper, Miss Lucy."

"Hey!" said a teenage girl, with a big smile. She had braces on her teeth that were the exact same light, bright blue color as her eyes.

Then the kids all went around and said their names. Amelia, who was in second grade. Lionel, third grade. Hayden, third. And Anton and Sparrow. They were the oldest.

"Today we're going to talk about prayer," said Miss Cathy. "Can anyone tell me how to pray?"

"Like this!" said Anton, clapping his hands together.

"Like that," agreed Miss Cathy. "And when you put your hands together, which finger is closest to you?"

Nobody answered.

"It's the thumb, isn't it?" said Miss Cathy. "So the first thing we pray for are the people closest to us. That might be your mom or dad, or your brother or sister. Okay? Next comes our pointer finger. It reminds us to pray for people who point us in the right direction, like your teachers."

Miss Cathy kept going. The tall finger reminded them to pray for those in authority, like the president of the United States. The next finger was for those who were suffering or in any sort of trouble. Then she held up her pinky finger. "And our little finger reminds us that we are small and God is great. When we get to the little finger, we ask for God's help. Any questions?"

Sparrow raised her hand. "What about animals?"

Miss Cathy smiled. "What about them?"

"Which finger is for animals? Is it on the other hand?"

"No, we only use one hand," said Miss Cathy.

"But you said to put your hands together," said Anton. "So there's five more fingers! Like, the thumb could be for dogs."

"Dinosaurs!" jumped in Hayden. "Can one finger be for dinosaurs?"

"They're extinct," said Lionel.

"You could pray for them to come back!" said Hayden.

"Sunday school friends!" said Miss Cathy. "We only use one hand to help us remember how to pray. But if you have an animal you want to pray for, go right ahead.

Now I want everyone to put their hand on their paper, and Miss Lucy will trace it, and you can color it in. And when you're done coloring, we'll have snack."

Coloring in your hand seemed like a craft activity for little kids. And Sparrow didn't really like people doing things for her that she could do herself. She could have traced her own hand. But while Miss Lucy was running a thick black marker around Sparrow's fingers, she said, in a low voice just for Sparrow, "I like your idea, to pray for animals," and Sparrow decided that if she ever had braces, she would get that light, bright blue color. She took a blue marker and began coloring.

Everyone had acted like going to church this morning was going to the moon. There were long discussions about who was doing what. Sparrow's dad was coming so he could drive them right up to the door and then go park the car. Sparrow's mom would stay with Mrs. LaRose, getting her out of the car and into the building. Sparrow wanted a job too, but everyone kept telling her to just stay out of the way. And Jenny wasn't coming with them. She was staying home to "get some things organized around here."

Suddenly Sparrow had a bad feeling. Other things Jenny LaRose had said popped into her head. *The best thing is for me to take the cats somewhere. . . . These cats are the biggest tripping hazard I ever saw.* What if the "things" Jenny was organizing were the cats? What if the organizing was taking them away to a shelter? What if she was doing that *right now*?

"Is it time for snack?" asked Amelia.

"Snack, snack, snack," chanted Lionel and Hayden and Anton.

Miss Cathy held up her hand. "Before we eat, who knows what it means to say grace?"

Amelia piped up. "It means saying thank you!"

"Exactly," said Miss Cathy. "Miss Lucy, you have a special grace for us, don't you?"

Miss Lucy nodded. "This grace is a song, and it goes to the tune of 'Pop Goes the Weasel.'" She sang:

> *Every day around this time,*
> *We gather at the table,*
> *But before we take a bite,*
> *We STOP and say thank you.*
> *Thanks to those who bought the food,*

Thanks to those who cooked it,
Most of all we thank you, Lord,
Now let's GO ahead and eat it!

They all sang along the second time around, and then they ate gluten-free crackers and drank apple juice from tiny paper cups, and then it was time to go join their parents for the rest of the service. Sparrow spotted them sitting in the front row beside Mrs. LaRose. She was easy to find because she had her walker parked in front of her. And on her head she wore a bright blue hat with a make-believe bird in a make-believe nest.

"Mom," whispered Sparrow. "How much longer?"

Sparrow's mom held out the leaflet that showed the order of the service and pointed: they were *here*. With nothing else to do but wait, Sparrow studied the leaflet. On the last page were announcements: "The Blessing of the Animals will be on the first Sunday in October. Please start collecting items for the Jumble Sale in November."

Sparrow didn't know how much longer church lasted. All she knew was it felt like forever. And forever was plenty of time for Jenny LaRose to make the cats disappear! But finally everyone was standing up to sing the last hymn. It was over. Except then there was something called coffee hour! Standing around in a big room while people came over to give Mrs. LaRose a hug.

There was lots of talk-talk-talking. Also, luckily, brownies. Then, *finally*, it was actually, really time to go.

Which was like another trip to the moon. Sparrow's dad went and got the car to drive it up to the door. Sparrow's mom guided Mrs. LaRose from the coffee hour room, through the church, to the front door. They got Mrs. LaRose into the car. Folded up the walker. Put it in the trunk.

Then Sparrow's dad drove slowly down Bridge Street and up Hartley Street. Pulled slowly into the parking spot alongside the house. And stopped the car. At last! Sparrow jumped from the car and raced up the ramp— bumping right into Jenny LaRose.

"Hey, slow down!" said Jenny.

"Sorry!" said Sparrow.

"You look like you're running for your life—is my mom okay? Mom!" she called as she hurried down the ramp toward the car. Leaving the door to Mrs. LaRose's wide open.

Alone, Sparrow slipped into the house. Into the kitchen. There was Pierre on the windowsill. Midnight on the comfy chair. Marmalade on the fridge. Sparrow felt like she had just run through a sprinkler. Relief washed over her like drops of water.

From outside, voices came drifting in, everybody on the ramp. "You're doing great" (Sparrow's mom). "I'll hold the door" (Sparrow's dad).

On the kitchen table sat a laptop. Sparrow took a step closer. She wasn't going to touch it. She was just going to look. Make sure Jenny wasn't researching animal shelters.

The voices were a little louder. Coming closer. "Do you want to rest?" (Jenny). "No, I don't need to rest!" (Mrs. LaRose).

Quickly Sparrow scanned the screen. *Saint Mary's Senior Living.* It wasn't a place for animals.

It was a place for people.

⤙ 22 ⤚

Sparrow whirled around to face the parade of grown-ups coming into the kitchen. Her feelings were swirling around too. Should she say something? Or pretend she hadn't seen anything, and say nothing? She wished she really hadn't seen the words "Saint Mary's Senior Living."

"Come on in, everyone," said Jenny LaRose. Brushing past Sparrow, she clapped the laptop shut and moved it off the table.

"We should probably go," said Sparrow's mom. "Come on, Sparrow."

"Actually," said Jenny, "can you stay a bit? I need to talk to everyone. I got doughnuts!" She cleared the kitty-cat salt and pepper shakers from the lazy Susan and set down a box of doughnuts.

"Doughnuts!" said Mrs. LaRose, trundling in with her walker. Then, slow and careful, she lowered herself into a chair. She took off her blue bird-in-a-nest hat and handed it to Jenny. "Did you get me a cinnamon cruller?"

"Of course, Mom! I know what your favorite doughnut is."

Everyone sat down except Jenny, who was bustling around pouring coffee for the grown-ups and a glass of cider for Sparrow. The cats did their usual things. Marmalade watched from the top of the fridge. Midnight kept snoozing in his spot. The tabbies jumped down from the windowsill and up onto laps. Pierre leapt onto Mrs. LaRose's lap, and Paulette leapt onto Sparrow's lap, then settled down with her white paws on Sparrow's bare knees. The only thing *not* usual was Mrs. Moon not rushing to Mrs. LaRose's side.

Sparrow whispered to Mrs. LaRose, "Where's Mrs. Moon?"

"She might be in her new bed," said Mrs. LaRose, adding, "Jenny bought it for her! It's right next to mine, in the other room."

"We'll get to that in a bit," said Jenny. "Everyone, help yourself."

What is that supposed to mean? wondered Sparrow as she picked a chocolate frosted.

When everyone had a drink and a doughnut, Jenny

finally sat down. But she still wasn't touching her dough-nut. So neither was Sparrow's mom or dad. So neither was Sparrow. There was a funny feeling in the room.

Mrs. LaRose turned to Sparrow. "What are we wait-ing for?"

Sparrow answered in a whisper, "Are we supposed to say grace?"

Everyone laughed and Sparrow felt stupid. She felt laughed at. How was she supposed to know when you did or didn't say grace? She ran her hand down Pau-lette's brown and black stripes, over and over. The tabby began purring and kneading her white paws into Sparrow's legs.

"I don't think you say grace for doughnuts," said her dad.

"We said it for snack in Sunday school," she said.

"That's a lovely idea," said Jenny. "Mom, will you?"

"Lord," said Mrs. LaRose, "we give you thanks for this beautiful autumn day, for friends and family. And for doughnuts. Amen."

They all echoed "Amen" and picked up their dough-nuts. Sparrow bit into her chocolate frosted. This whole grace thing was confusing. When you said it. What you said. Apparently, you could sing or say a ready-made grace. Or you could make something up.

"So," began Jenny. "We need to tell you something. My mom is moving down to Massachusetts, where I live."

"Wow," said Sparrow's mom. "That's . . . big news!"

"Really big," agreed Sparrow's dad.

The news was so big, it started taking up all the room in Sparrow's stomach. She had the feeling she got when she spun too long on the spinner at the playground. She put her one-bite-taken-out doughnut back on her napkin.

"First of all," said Jenny, "I want to say that I am so sorry about the ramp! But I thought my mom would be here for a while longer. I had put her name down for a facility really close to my house. But it had a long waiting list. They said it could be months! Then yesterday they called. They have an unexpected opening. It's getting a fresh coat of paint, but it will be ready in a week. It just seemed like the right thing at the right time."

Sparrow turned to her dad. "You said she could keep living here!" she blurted. "That's what you *said!*"

He made a *This is all news to me* face.

Mrs. LaRose spoke up. "I was," she said. "That was the plan when your parents bought the house. I would stay here, at least for a while. But now—it's time."

"Of course you two want to be close," said Sparrow's mom. "That's the important thing. We understand. Don't we, Sparrow?"

Sparrow hated it when her mom said "we" like that. Including her. Because "we" didn't understand at all. So the Sparrow part of "we" refused to answer.

Jenny filled in the awkward silence of Sparrow not answering. "It's a really nice facility," she said. "She'll have her own space, but I can pop over anytime. And it's all on one level—no stairs."

"And they let you have pets!" added Mrs. LaRose.

"Well, that's great!" said Sparrow's mom.

"Pets?" asked Sparrow's fact-checking dad. "Or *a pet?"*

"One pet," clarified Jenny.

"One?" Sparrow cried. "What about all the others?"

"That's the trouble," said Mrs. LaRose, dropping her gaze and slowly stroking the tabby in her lap. Her white braids crisscrossed over the top of her head. "That's what I'm worried about."

"Oh my goodness," said Sparrow's mom. "Six cats that need homes."

"Actually," said Jenny, "the problem is bigger than six cats."

"What do you mean?" asked Sparrow's dad.

"I'm surprised nobody noticed," said Jenny. "But it looks to me like Mrs. Moon is going to have kittens."

⸙ 23 ⸙

"**K**ittens?" cried Sparrow.

"Kittens?" echoed her mom and dad.

"Kittens," said Jenny LaRose.

"Kittens," agreed Mrs. LaRose. "It's a little bit my fault, I'm afraid. She was a stray, you know. I should have taken her to the vet to make sure she was spayed. But I never did!"

"Who knows?" said Sparrow's dad. "She might have been pregnant already when you found her."

"That's true," said Mrs. LaRose. "But still . . . ," she started, then stopped, turning to Sparrow. "That's one of the reasons I agreed it's time. The house and all the cats. It's too much for me now."

"What's so bad about Mrs. Moon having kittens?" asked Sparrow.

Sparrow's mom cleared her throat. "It's just better for these things to be on purpose. Planned. That way you know there are people who will love them and give them a good home."

"Everybody loves kittens," objected Sparrow.

"Well, not everybody," corrected her dad. "Some people are allergic."

"Like my daughter," said Jenny. "That's why my mom isn't going to live with me. At Saint Mary's, she can keep one cat and come visit me whenever she wants. And my daughter can come over and not worry about her breathing."

"And someday," added Mrs. LaRose, "the baby can come!"

"That's our other news," said Jenny LaRose. "My daughter is going to have a baby. I'm going to be a grandmother!"

"I'm going to be a great-grandmother!" said Mrs. LaRose, doing a little in-her-seat dance, her bottom half staying put but her arms swaying back and forth.

"That's great news!" said Sparrow's dad.

"Speaking of babies," said Sparrow's mom, "maybe this is a good time to share that I'm going to have a baby too!"

All the grown-ups began trading questions about babies and due dates. Which did not interest Sparrow. At. All. "Can I go look for Mrs. Moon?" she asked.

"Sure," said Jenny. "Try down the hall."

Sparrow gave Paulette a little nudge, and the tabby leapt off her lap. She headed down the hall, past the clock, into what used to be the living room. Now the sofa was pushed into a corner, and in the middle of the room sat the hospital bed. On one side of the bed was a little table covered with a lace doily. On the other side was a basket with a big pillow inside, and Mrs. Moon stretched out on the pillow.

Sparrow plunked herself down on the floor and ran her hand from the top of Mrs. Moon's head down to the tip of her tail, over and over. She still had the feeling of going too long on the spinner at the playground. Even after you got off, it felt like the world kept spinning. Her head was spinning too, with questions.

Which cat would Mrs. LaRose take with her? And what would happen to all the other cats—would Jenny LaRose send them all to the animal shelter? And how many kittens would Mrs. Moon have? And what would happen to *them*?

The clock began gonging. Sparrow liked counting the gongs, but you had to think quick. The second you heard the first one, you had to start counting. One, two, three, four, five, six, seven, eight, nine, ten, eleven, twelve. It was twelve o'clock.

"Sparrow!" her mom called from down the hall. "We need to get going! Five-minute warning!"

Five-minute warnings were part of "positive parent-ing" so that nobody (meaning Sparrow) felt surprised in a bad way. Stroking Mrs. Moon's soft white fur, Sparrow called "Got it!" just like she was supposed to. So that nobody (meaning her parents) felt like she wasn't being a cooperator.

A five-minute warning meant she had to think quick. She had five minutes to come up with a plan. A plan to save the cats from going to the shelter. And maybe—just maybe—talk her parents into letting her keep a kitten.

⤚ 24 ⤙

The five minutes were up, and Sparrow had nothing. No plan. But she wasn't going to let that stop her. Back in the kitchen with everyone, she asked, "What about the cats Mrs. LaRose doesn't take? What's going to happen to them?"

"They can go to the Eastbrook Animal Shelter," said Jenny, "and I'm sure somebody will adopt them."

"That is so unfair!" said Sparrow. "Why should they have to go there? They'll probably be in little cages! What if they have to spend their whole day in there? What if they can never go outside? They would hate that! How would *you* like to live in a little cage?"

Sparrow's parents tag-teamed her.

"That's enough," said her dad. "It's not your decision."

"That's more than enough," agreed her mom. Then she added, "I'm so sorry. I think someone's having a brownie-at-church-and-then-a-doughnut sugar melt-down."

Sparrow hated it when her mom apologized for her. You shouldn't be allowed to apologize for somebody else. She *wasn't* sorry. Somebody needed to stick up for the cats. And she hated it when her mom said she was having a sugar meltdown. You shouldn't be allowed to say that when somebody is really, truly, actually upset for a perfectly good reason. Besides, she hadn't even finished her doughnut! She'd taken only one bite!

"I'm serious!" she cried. "Why can't we just keep them? I can take care of them—you know I can! I did it the whole time Mrs. LaRose wasn't here."

"You did a wonderful job," said Mrs. LaRose.

"And we're grateful," added Jenny LaRose.

"But we are not adopting seven cats," said her mom.

"It's only six," said Sparrow. "Mrs. LaRose is taking one."

"Six cats," said her dad, getting the facts straight, "but who knows how many kittens?"

"The answer is no, Sparrow," said her mom. "We are not keeping the cats. They'll go to the shelter. End of story."

No way. That could not be the end of the story. Just

because they couldn't keep the cats didn't mean they should go live in cages. But while Sparrow was searching for a eureka-moment great idea to convince everybody, her dad rose from his chair.

"I think we better get going," he said.

"I think so too," her mom said, standing as well and putting her hand on Sparrow's shoulder. "Time to say goodbye, Sparrow."

"No!" cried Sparrow.

All she meant to do was get her mom's hand off her. Because she didn't want to be touched, or hugged, or guided out of the room. But somehow she pushed off her mom's hand so hard that her own hand kept flying through the air. And suddenly her glass was being knocked off the table and falling to the floor. It landed with a thud, and for a second everyone seemed frozen.

Mrs. LaRose spoke first. "It's not broken," she said. "And it wasn't even full, so nothing spilled. So let's not get our panties twisted in a knot, people!"

And instead of her parents scolding her, they started laughing. And while they were laughing, Sparrow started to get her idea. The glass falling off the table reminded her of the day she and her dad had gone to the bakery, and by accident she had knocked a coffee cup off the table. Because of the lady with the jean jacket. The lady who had just wanted to get home. Because everybody just wanted to get home, right?

She asked, "What if I find homes for them?"

Nobody said no right away. Nobody was shutting her down. Everybody was listening. So she kept going.

"What if I find people who want to adopt them? But the cats can stay here until I do? I can ask kids at school, and I can ask people at church. I bet lots of people there would want one of Mrs. LaRose's cats!"

Sparrow watched as her mom and dad traded *What do you think? No, what do* you *think?* glances. Then her mom said out loud to Jenny, "What do you think?"

"I don't know," said Jenny, shaking her head. "It seems like a big job for a little kid."

"Well, I think it's genius," said Mrs. LaRose. "And if Sparrow's parents agree, then we do too." She made a fist and set it on the table, as if it was decided.

Sparrow's mom drew a deep breath. "All right," she agreed. *"But*—you can't go about this all willy-nilly." And she and Sparrow's dad proceeded to lay down a bunch of rules.

Sparrow could conduct her search "old-school." That meant asking people she knew. In person. She could ask kids at school, or people at church, or neighbors on Hartley Street. But no posting on the internet because they did not want Sparrow fielding a bunch of emails from strangers.

Also, the search couldn't go on forever. Sparrow had one month to find homes for the cats. Same for the kittens after they were born. If she hadn't found homes for them all in a month, well, "we'll see."

Sparrow was still not a fan of "we'll see." She decided she just wouldn't think about that part.

~ 25 ~

The next morning it was raining. Sparrow sploshed her way to school. *Splosh* was the sound her boots made when she stepped in a puddle. There were two ways to splosh. Dance-sploshing was for dancing in the puddles, and stomp-sploshing was for stomping.

Dance-sploshing was for happy steps. Because she was going to find homes for the cats. And because—kittens! And because in the fight between the cat-loving butterfly dancers and the plodding-along grown-ups, the dancers had won. Mrs. LaRose had insisted that while she was still in her house, she wanted Sparrow to come over in the afternoons. And everyone had agreed.

Stomp-sploshing was for mad steps. Because she wanted to tell Paloma everything, but how was she supposed to do that when they basically weren't talking to each other?

Halfway down Hartley Street she sploshed past the Randolphs' house, where the ladybug flag was getting wet. Anton stepped outside. "Hey, wait up!" he called, running to catch up. Sparrow waited, and they began walking to school together.

"I heard about the kittens!" he said.

"What? How?"

"Your mom called my mom to say that you weren't coming over this week after school. And my mom asked why, and your mom told her the whole story."

"Anton, you better not blab this time. I'm serious."

"What?" he asked in a phony *I don't know what you mean* voice.

Somehow Sparrow was going to try to fix things with Paloma. And she had no idea if telling Paloma about all the things she had found out yesterday was going to help. But she knew that Anton telling was *not* going to help.

"Do *not* tell Paloma," she said. "I'm going to tell her."

"Okay, whatever," said Anton.

"Promise," she demanded.

"Okay, okay," he said. "I promise."

When they got to school, Sparrow trudged in with all the other kids in rain boots and raincoats. The halls had a rainy, wet-sock smell. Outside Mrs. Foxworthy's room, she hung up her raincoat in her locker and waited in the hall as long as she could, hoping to talk to Paloma. But Paloma arrived late, just as morning announcements were beginning. She slipped into her seat, turning sideways in her chair so she wasn't facing Sparrow.

"Good morning, Eastbrook Elementary!" said Principal Weiss over the intercom.

There was news about lunch (chicken nuggets or falafel) and birthday wishes (Nadia Melton), and then came the recording of kids saying good morning. *"Buenos días, sabah al-khair, bonjour . . ."* After announcements Mrs. Foxworthy asked everyone to take out a piece of paper and a pencil. They were going to spend ten minutes writing about something they had seen or done that weekend.

Sparrow had missed the chance to talk to Paloma alone before school. Lunchtime was too far away, and besides, the cafeteria would be crowded and noisy. She had no choice. This called for a note.

In tiny letters she wrote the word *Sorry*. Which didn't seem like enough. She added, *sorry sorry sorry sorry!* She didn't have time or room to explain the whole story, so she wrote, *Recess?* Then she finished with a smiley face and the word *KITTENS!*

She folded up the paper as small as she could. Now came the question, Which way to pass it? Sparrow's desk was in one corner of the blue pod, with Paloma diagonally across from her, and Anton and Caleb were between them. She could try flicking the note right across the pod to Paloma. Too risky. She'd have to get Anton or Caleb to pass it. But Anton might flub it on purpose, just for fun. So that left Caleb, who was busy scribbling, working on the assignment. Probably writing about all the creatures he had slayed in *Earthwatch Invasion.*

Slowly she slid the tiny, folded-up note from her desk onto his. But he was so busy writing, he didn't notice.

"Caleb," she whispered. *"Caleb."*

Still no response. The note was just sitting there. She had to do something. Under cover of the desks, she used her pencil to nudge him on the leg.

Startled, Caleb pivoted toward her. His arm swept across his desk. The note flew into the middle of the room and dropped to the floor.

Mrs. Foxworthy walked over toward the blue pod. The room had an electric feeling, as if the flash of white had been a bolt of lightning, not just a piece of folded-up paper. Nineteen kids stopped what they were doing. Everyone who had seen the note and where it had come from was busy whispering to anyone who hadn't seen it.

Mrs. Foxworthy picked the note up off the floor and dropped it on her desk.

"Everyone, please keep working," she said, "and, Sparrow, please see me briefly at recess."

Somebody's in trouble noises rumbled through the room like thunder after lightning, and Sparrow stared down at her hands in her lap. When she looked up, the kids in her pod all had their eyes on her.

Anton just looked like he was enjoying the action. Caleb mouthed the word "sorry." And Paloma, finally, didn't have that stony look on her face anymore. Her eyes were wide open. Curious. Like she wanted to know what was in that note.

⚹ 26 ⚹

Sparrow picked a chocolate milk box from the case and made her way through the lunch line. She had spent the morning wondering what Mrs. Foxworthy was going to say to her after lunch, at recess. But now she had a bigger problem. Today was the first day kids had been released from their assigned tables. Foxworthy fourth graders didn't have to sit together anymore. So where was she going to sit?

Gripping her tray, Sparrow looked around. Everywhere kids were sorting themselves into groups. Kids who were in different classes but were friends because they played on the same team. Kids who were in different classes but were friends because they'd been in the same class last year. Now they could sit together.

Sparrow didn't have any old friends here, and the

only new one she had made wasn't speaking to her. So where was she supposed to sit?

One of the cafeteria ladies had the same question. "Where are you sitting, dear?"

"I don't know," said Sparrow.

"There's a seat," said the cafeteria lady, pointing to a table. "Take it, dear, or you won't have time to eat."

It was a table of fourth-grade girls. There were a few girls Sparrow didn't know, from another class. From Mrs. Foxworthy's class there were Harriet and Yasmeen from the green pod, and Anna from the yellow pod. And there was Paloma, sitting in the middle, her kitty-cat headband on top of her head like it was a crown and she was the queen of the table.

Sparrow set down her tray at the very end of the table. "Hey," she said to no one in particular.

"Hey," said Harriet, with a little wave of her hand. On her wrist were a bunch of sparkly hair elastics. Her fun fact had been that she'd won first place in the Maine junior gymnastics meet. Sparrow had seen her do a handspring on the playground, her long ponytail whirling as she flipped around.

"Hey," echoed Yasmeen, with a little wave too and a smile. She wore a hijab dotted with leopard paw prints, and her fun fact had been that she was getting a cell phone for her next birthday.

Anna and Paloma silently lifted their hands. Kind

of saying hey. But kind of not. The girls from the other class all followed their lead, glancing at Sparrow, then turning back to their lunches and their conversations.

"So," said Harriet, "are you in trouble?"

"I don't know," said Sparrow. Because she didn't know what Mrs. Foxworthy was going to say yet.

"Do you have indoor recess?" asked Yasmeen.

"I don't know," said Sparrow. Because Mrs. Foxworthy had only said to see her at recess, not that she would spend the whole recess inside.

Anna drew a sandwich from her lunch bag. Her fun fact had been that she was taking riding lessons, and she wore her hair in one of those woven braids, like on the mane of a horse. "Do you know *anything*?" she asked.

Faces swiveled toward Sparrow. All the girls began paying attention now. A few of them giggled. Not Paloma, though. She was looking at Sparrow, but she wasn't laughing.

Sometimes Sparrow studied the face of one of the cats. Sometimes she felt sure they wanted to speak. But they just couldn't. She had the same feeling now. Like maybe Paloma wanted to say something, but she couldn't.

"What did you do?" asked one of the girls from the other class.

"She passed a note!" said Harriet.

"She *tried* to pass a note," corrected Yasmeen. "And Mrs. Foxworthy got it!"

Anna leaned toward Paloma, whispering. Paloma was still gazing at Sparrow like a cat that couldn't speak. Maybe it was like one of those fairy tales where somebody is trapped under a spell. They can't speak until the spell gets broken.

"So," said Anna, with a *Dare you* note in her voice, "who was it for?"

Sparrow didn't want to be in one of Anton's fights. Anna vs. Sparrow. But she did want to break the spell Paloma seemed to be under.

"Paloma," she said. *"Obviously."*

Harriet and Yasmeen and all the other girls pivoted toward Paloma, who had a big grin on her face now.

"I knew it!" she said. "Caleb is such a doofus."

"It wasn't his fault," said Sparrow. "He couldn't help it. I scared him by mistake."

That was it. It wasn't a lot of words, but everything felt different. It felt like the cold silence was over. And suddenly Sparrow felt so thirsty. She picked up her chocolate milk box and glugged down a big swallow. Paloma picked up her chocolate milk box and drank too.

Anna wasn't giving up so easily. "So what did it say?" she demanded.

Sparrow set down her milk box. With her thirst

quenched, she had a new feeling. Silly. Super silly. She pinched her nose between her thumb and pointer finger. And in a nose-squeezed-shut, funny-sounding voice she said, *"'Sorry sorry sorry sorry sorry!' And . . . 'KITTENS!'"*

Paloma spluttered chocolate milk all over the place, gasping for breath and laughing at the same time. "Kittens?" she cried when she could talk.

"Kittens," said Sparrow.

⊁ 27 ⊁

It was still raining after lunch, which meant indoor recess.

"Welcome back," said Mrs. Foxworthy, with her red glasses perched on top of her head. "These are the choices. We have LEGOs at this station and art supplies at this station. Over here is my rainy-day box with some magazines and puzzles. Or you can pick a book for free reading."

There were groans from the kids who hated to be inside and cheers from the kids who liked to read. Then came the moment. The *See me* moment. With a little wave of her hand, Mrs. Foxworthy beckoned Sparrow over.

Sparrow stepped up to the teacher's desk, bracing herself for a lecture. Or a consequence. Or both. But all that came next was Mrs. Foxworthy handing her the folded-up note. "I think you dropped this," she said, and added, "Looks like somebody's waiting for you."

From across the room, Paloma was waving.

Sparrow felt a rush of gratitude. "Sorry," she said, dropping the note in the wastebasket next to Mrs. Foxworthy's desk. She didn't need it anymore.

She headed over to the art station, where Paloma was drawing pictures of cats.

"Those are good!" said Sparrow. "Could you draw all of Mrs. LaRose's cats?"

"Sure," said Paloma. "How come?"

Quickly she filled Paloma in on the rest of the story—Mrs. LaRose moving, the cats needing new homes—and they started making a poster.

Wanted: homes for cats. Sparrow wrote down the name of each cat, with a description, and Paloma drew a little picture of each one with colored pencils.

Marmalade: Orange tabby.

Midnight: All black. Likes to sleep a lot.

Tuxedo: Black with white throat and paws. Friendly.

Pierre: Brown-and-black tabby. Very friendly. Would like to stay with Paulette.

Paulette: Brown-and-black tabby with white paws. Friendly. Would like to stay with Pierre.

Kitty Gray: All gray. Likes to go outside.

Mrs. Moon: All white. Very soft, very friendly. Needs home later.

Sparrow hadn't been sure about putting all seven cats on the poster. Because Mrs. LaRose was taking one. She hadn't said which one, though. So for now they put all of them on.

Outside, the rain kept falling, rolling down the windows. Inside, Mrs. Foxworthy was strolling from station to station, checking in.

"What are you working on, girls?"

Sparrow showed her the paper: *Wanted: homes for cats.*

"Oh. My. Goodness," said Mrs. Foxworthy. "Is this for real? Because I've actually been thinking about getting a cat, and I have always wanted an orange tabby."

"Seriously?" asked Sparrow.

"Seriously," said Mrs. Foxworthy, nodding, her red glasses bobbing up and down with each nod. "Why don't you check Marmalade off your list?"

Sparrow put a big X over the picture of Marmalade.

"And while you're at it, do you want to put this out to the class?"

"Like—how?" asked Sparrow.

"By standing up and sharing it. Just briefly. You never know, you might find another home. What do you think?"

"You totally should!" said Paloma.

What Sparrow thought was that she totally should. Except for one thing. She didn't love the idea of reminding everyone that the cats weren't hers. That she had lied about her fun fact. But she *did* love the idea of finding homes for the cats.

"What do you say?" asked Mrs. Foxworthy, putting a hand on Sparrow's shoulder. Mrs. Foxworthy, who hadn't scolded her. And who was going to adopt Marmalade. "Ready to do this?"

Sparrow gave a quick nod and stood up.

"Fourth graders!" called Mrs. Foxworthy. "Can Sparrow have your attention?"

Everybody looked up from what they were doing. Anton and Caleb from the LEGO table. Harriet and Yasmeen from the cat's cradle strung between their hands. Anna from the book she was reading.

Sparrow felt her face growing hot and sort of buzzy, like when she hung upside down on the monkey bars for too long. Like if she couldn't pull herself back upright, she might fall on her head.

"I don't have seven cats," she blurted. "I said I did. For my fun fact. But I don't. They aren't mine. They belong to my neighbor, but she has to move, and the cats need homes. And I'm trying to find homes for them so they don't have to go to a shelter. So if anybody wants to take a cat, come see me."

Mrs. Foxworthy gave her a big smile and a thumbs-up. Sparrow took a deep breath and sat back down. She was on solid ground again. Right side up. She had told everyone the whole story. And maybe somebody would take a cat!

"Hey," said Paloma. "What about the kittens? Should we put them on the poster too?"

"No," said Sparrow, shaking her head. "'Cause we don't even know how many there will be."

"And I want one," said Paloma. "If my mom says yes, I can have one, right?"

Sparrow didn't want to mess things up with Paloma again by making a promise she couldn't keep. Maybe she should say "maybe." Or "probably." She could say "probably."

"Definitely!" she said.

⤜ 28 ⤙

Before the end of school, the rain stopped and the sun came out. On the walk home everything felt washed and clean. The trees had just had a shower. The sidewalks had just had a bath. All that was left of the rain were some puddles, which Sparrow dance-sploshed in all the way home. She galloped up the ramp onto the porch, tugged off her rain boots, and peeled off her wet socks. Barefoot, she hurried inside.

"*Bienvenue!*" cried Mrs. LaRose.

"Guess what?" said Sparrow. "I told my class about the cats, and kids are going to ask their parents, and Paloma says she might take a kitten, and my teacher can take Marmalade!"

"Do you hear that, Marmalade?" asked Mrs. LaRose. "You've been chosen."

From the top of the fridge, Marmalade gazed down at them with a haughty air. He blinked his eyes.

"He's saying, 'Of course I'm chosen, I'm so awesome,'" said Sparrow.

"Come and sit," said Mrs. LaRose, pointing to the table, where a pitcher of lemonade stood and a plate of cookies sat. "We have peanut butter cookies."

Sparrow flung her backpack onto one chair and plopped herself down onto another. Done. It took Mrs. LaRose a lot longer. Gripping her walker, she trundled over to the kitchen table. Pivoted around so the chair was behind her. Lowered herself onto the seat. Seeing their chance, the tabbies jumped down from the windowsill and came over. Finally Sparrow and Mrs. LaRose were both settled down with lemonade and cookies and cats in their laps.

Sparrow unzipped her backpack and pulled out the little-bit-crumpled poster. "Look what I made," she said.

Mrs. LaRose studied the poster. "These are wonderful! Pierre and Paulette, look!" she said to the tabbies. "There you are!"

"I know, they're really good! Paloma drew them," Sparrow said, and added, "She's my best friend."

Saying those words gave her a sun-coming-out-after-the-rain feeling. But then a cloud came back.

Paloma was definitely *her* best friend. But was she Paloma's? Just because they had made up, it might not mean Paloma wanted to be *best* friends. Or even if she did, she might want to stay friends with Anna, too. Sparrow took another cookie and nibbled it, thinking. The best thing would be one best friend you didn't have to share. But what if that wasn't a choice? What if the choices were no best friend—like last week—or sharing your best friend? She didn't like those choices. She popped the rest of the cookie in her mouth and took another.

"I didn't know which cat to leave off, though. Which cat you're taking with you."

"I don't know either," said Mrs. LaRose. "I'm in a pickle, for sure."

They ticked off the cats. Mrs. LaRose wouldn't choose Marmalade, since he was already spoken for. She wouldn't choose Pierre and Paulette, since she could have only one cat, and hopefully those two were staying together. And perhaps it would be better not to choose Kitty Gray, since whichever cat she took would have to be an inside cat, and Kitty Gray would hate that. That left Midnight, Tuxedo, or Mrs. Moon.

Sparrow pointed to Midnight, gazing at them from his spot on the comfy chair. "He's saying, 'I won't make any trouble at all. Choose me!'"

Mrs. LaRose pointed to Tuxedo, sitting in a patch of sunlight, licking his paws and rubbing them against his head to clean himself. "He's saying, 'I'm so handsome and I keep myself so nice. Choose me.'"

Now Mrs. Moon wandered into the kitchen and over to the bowl of water. The white cat drank, then came and made some figure eights around Mrs. LaRose's ankles, before padding back out again.

"Oh dear," said Mrs. LaRose. "I could never choose."

"Choices are hard," agreed Sparrow.

"I'm not going to choose," declared Mrs. LaRose. "I'll let others choose, and take whichever cat is left at the end."

"That would have to be Mrs. Moon, though, right?" asked Sparrow. "Because she has to stay here until the kittens are born."

"Yes, probably Mrs. Moon."

Just then the phone started to ring.

"Sparrow," said Mrs. LaRose, pointing across the room to the black phone stuck to the wall. "Will you get that? Jenny is out running errands, and by the time I get there . . ."

By the time Mrs. LaRose hauled herself up to standing and shuffled her walker over to the phone—which rang a second time—the person calling would probably have hung up.

Sparrow gave Paulette a nudge, and the tabby jumped off her lap and onto the floor. The phone rang a third time before she got there. It rang once more as she hesitated. With this phone there was no way to know who was on the other end. It was just a black box with a long, curly cord that connected to a receiver, which she picked up. "Hello?"

"Hello, Mrs. LaRose? It's Megan, over at the church."

"Just a sec, I'll get her," said Sparrow, stepping toward Mrs. LaRose.

The long, curly cord attaching the stuck-on-the-wall part of the phone to the receiver uncurled. Stretched. But not far enough. Old phones were weird, thought Sparrow. It was like you were on a leash!

Mrs. LaRose seemed to see the problem. "Who is it?" she asked.

"Megan, from church."

"The church secretary," explained Mrs. LaRose, circling her hand in the air a couple of times, as if to say, *Keep going*. "Ask her what she wants."

So Sparrow began telling Mrs. LaRose what the church secretary said, and telling the church secretary what Mrs. LaRose said. It was kind of like a game of telephone—with an actual telephone.

Megan: The church had heard that Mrs. LaRose was moving soon, and they were planning a festive coffee hour in her honor. They wanted to make sure she would be there this Sunday.

Mrs. LaRose: Yes, but she didn't want any fuss. Well, maybe a little fuss was okay.

Sparrow didn't mind playing telephone, but she did mind standing still. As she talked, she walked back and forth. And as she walked back and forth, the cord went from stretched straight out to curly and dangling down.

Megan: Wonderful! They would see her Sunday. "And thank you for your help, . . ."

Sparrow filled in the blank. "Sparrow," she answered, giving the dangling cord a swing.

"Thank you, Sparrow," said Megan.

Suddenly two things happened at the same time. The clock began sounding the hour, and Midnight—the cat who never budged—budged. First gong: he jumped off the comfy chair. Second gong: he leapt toward the swinging cord. Third gong: he began batting the cord with his paws. Fourth and last gong, four o'clock: Sparrow saw what to do. Black cat. Usually-sleepy-but-sometimes-crazy cat. Cat that needed a home.

"Wait!" she said. "Can you put something else in the leaflet?"

"You got it," said Megan. "Hit me."

Cats, explained Sparrow. Five of Mrs. LaRose's cats needed homes. So if anybody could adopt one of them, they should see Sparrow or her mom or dad at coffee

hour. Then she said thanks and goodbye. Hung up the phone. Tossed another peanut butter cookie in her mouth and washed it down with a slug of lemonade, imagining her parents congratulating her. Finding homes for all the cats? No problem! Sparrow took care of everything.

That was just Sparrow being Sparrow.

⤙ 29 ⤚

The next day Sparrow had choir practice,
which her mom had made her sign up for because
"it might be fun." In Sparrow's experience, being told
something "might be fun" was pretty much a guarantee
it wouldn't be. But there was no way out. When it was
her mom and Anton's mom vs. anybody else, who would
win? The moms.

After school Sparrow and Anton walked together
to the church on Bridge Street. They had a long list of
instructions. First, *stay together*. Second, remember
that Amelia from Sunday school was going to be in
the choir, and her mom would be there if they needed
anything. Third, walk home together afterward.

In the music room they found a bunch of kids running around, a couple of moms tapping on their cell

phones, and the choir director sitting at a piano. He wore perfectly round Harry Potter glasses and a grass-green bow tie.

"Hello, hello," he said to Sparrow and Anton, and he began playing a few notes on the piano. First he played something fast. Then he played something slow. The running kids slowed down. He kept playing with one hand, holding his other hand up in the air. Everyone knew what a raised hand meant, from school: *Stop*. One by one the running kids came to a stop.

"Thank you," said the choir director. "To begin, I am Mr. Parker, and you may call me Mr. Parker. Now tell me who you all are...."

They went around saying their names. There were seven kids altogether. Sparrow. Anton. Amelia from their Sunday school class. Amelia's two older sisters, Sadie and Becca, who were twins in the fifth grade at Eastbrook. And Daniel and Nathaniel, two boys who looked like they were brothers, with matching buzz cuts.

For the next half hour they sang. After they did some scales, they sang rounds. Sparrow stood on one side of the piano with Amelia and Sadie and Daniel. On the other side were Anton and Becca and Nathaniel. Mr. Parker was able to play piano and signal to each group at the same time. Pointing: *Start now*. Wrapping his fingers in a fist: *Now stop*.

They sang "Row, Row, Row Your Boat," which everybody knew. They sang "Make New Friends." And they sang "I Like the Flowers." Sparrow liked the part that went "boom-dee-ah-da, boom-dee-ah-da, boom-dee-ah-da, boom-dee-ah-da." And she liked the way rounds went around and around, like the lazy Susan on Mrs. LaRose's kitchen table. Here came the salt-and-pepper cats; here came the sugar. Here came the flowers; here came the "boom-dee-ah-da."

Mr. Parker pointed at Sparrow's group and drew his hand into a fist, and they sang the last "boom-dee-ah-da."

"Not! Bad!" he said. "Not bad at all! Now, the pastor has asked us to sing at a special service in a couple of weeks. I'm afraid that is not much time to learn a song, but we will do our best. Who knows the next holiday we celebrate?"

"Christmas!" shouted Daniel.

"Sooner than that," said Mr. Parker.

"Halloween?" tried Nathaniel.

"Sooner than that," said Mr. Parker. "In October we honor Saint Francis, who loved animals. Who was here last year and remembers the Blessing of the Animals?"

"I do," said Anton. "We had dogs in church!"

"Correct," said Mr. Parker. "We had dogs. We had cats. Somebody brought their snake."

Becca piped up, "My little sister brought her goldfish!"

Sadie added, "And the pastor held it up in front of everybody!"

"I remember!" said Mr. Parker. "Are you going to bring your goldfish again, Amelia?"

Amelia didn't answer.

"Uh-oh," said Sadie, just as Amelia started crying.

"Her fish died," added Becca.

Amelia's mom slipped over to the piano, plucked a tissue from a box nearby, and handed it to Amelia. She used it to smear her tears all over her face.

"I am so sorry," said Mr. Parker. "I know how much it hurts to lose a pet." He began playing a few notes on the piano, then stopped. "The same thing happened to me. Last year I brought my precious Coco. . . ."

He broke off, and for a moment there was silence. Nobody talked. Nobody sang. Nobody played the piano. In the silence Sparrow started to have a funny feeling that Mr. Parker might be . . . *crying*. Not little-kid crying, with lots of snot. Crying you couldn't hear and could hardly see. He reached behind his round glasses and touched a fingertip to the corner of his eye.

Sparrow couldn't keep not-talking and not-singing and not-doing-anything. She had to do *something*. She tugged a tissue from the box and handed it to him.

Holding the tissue to his nose, he made a huge, honking trumpet sound. "Thank you," he said, waving the tissue in her direction, as if he was signaling, *I can't remember your name.*

"Sparrow."

"Thank you, Sparrow." He made the trumpet noise again. Cleared his throat. Took a deep breath. "Now let's give this song a try. I'll sing the chorus through once."

> *All things bright and beautiful,*
> *All creatures great and small.*
> *All things wise and wonderful,*
> *The Lord God made them all.*

Part of Sparrow's brain was listening. But another part was wondering: What if Coco had been a cat? Thinking: if Coco had been a cat, maybe Mr. Parker would want another. Deciding: as soon as choir practice ended, she would ask him if he wanted to adopt a cat.

⤜ 30 ⤛

Meals on the weekend were a big deal in the Robinson house. Since her parents worked different shifts during the week, it was the only time they all sat down together to eat. Her parents had even dressed up a little. Her dad had put on a button-down shirt, and her mom wore a flowered blouse. The windows were open, and the not-too-hot, not-too-cool air of September floated into the kitchen.

Sparrow took her seat. "Hungry!" she said, lifting up her plate. "So. Hungry. Please. Help."

"All right, Little Bird," said Sparrow's mom, serving up the spaghetti.

When Sparrow's mom called her Little Bird, it meant she was in a good mood. Which was a good thing, because tonight Sparrow was going to make her case.

"But before we start," added her mom, "what if we tried to say grace tonight?"

Sparrow's dad put down his fork. "Good idea," he said. "I like it."

Spaghetti smell was rising off the plate in front of Sparrow, going right into her nose. She wanted to eat. Right *now*. But if she was going to keep being "Little Bird" instead of "Sparrow!" she had to be a cooperator. Not a grumpus drama queen.

"Miss Lucy sang one in Sunday school," she said. "But I forget how it goes."

"Is that your teacher?" asked her dad.

"She's not the teacher, she's the helper. She has blue braces. Can I have blue braces?"

"Let's pray you don't need braces at all," said her mom. "But if you need them, sure, why not? But back to grace."

"Mrs. LaRose just winged it," said her dad.

"Winging it sounds like a job for a little bird," said Sparrow's mom. "Want to try, Sparrow?"

Sparrow thought winging it might be easier if she could stand on a chair and jump down, but that was a no go. She tried to think of something grace-y to say, but all she could think about was the smell of spaghetti. It smelled so good. And she was so hungry. Then she remembered what little Amelia had said in Sunday school. Saying grace just meant saying thanks.

"Thank you for spaghetti, God," she said. That didn't seem like enough, so she added, "I *love* spaghetti, so thanks a *lot*." That couldn't be good enough, could it? But when she looked at her parents, they had big smiles on their faces.

"Nice," said her dad. "Honest. To the point."

"And heartfelt," said her mom.

Everyone dug into their food.

"What a week," said Sparrow's dad. "I'm going to be honest—I didn't know if you could do it. But you did. You found homes for the cats."

"Six cats," added her mom. "In five days. It feels like a miracle."

They went over the miracle, cat by cat.

On Monday, Mrs. Foxworthy had offered to take Marmalade.

On Tuesday, Mr. Parker, the choir director, had agreed to take Pierre and Paulette.

On Wednesday, the neighbor with the sprinkler (whose name was Mrs. Snyder) came over to say that since Kitty Gray already spent a lot of time in her house, she would love to adopt her for good.

On Thursday, Caleb from the blue pod said his parents would let him take Tuxedo.

And on Friday, Mrs. Randolph said that they couldn't have a cat because one of her day care kids had allergies. But her sister—Anton's aunt Mary—could take Midnight.

And today, Saturday, six cats had gone to their new homes. Everyone came over and picked up the cats they had chosen. Only Mrs. Snyder didn't need to actually come over because she lived right next door and Kitty Gray was already at her house.

Just like that, the cats were gone. All except Mrs. Moon. She was the one Mrs. LaRose was going to keep.

Sparrow heard her parents going over the rest of Mrs. LaRose's moving plans, which she already knew by heart. So mostly she was busy twirling spaghetti around her fork, then trying to get the whole twirled-up swirl into her mouth.

Tomorrow, right after church, Jenny and Mrs. LaRose were heading to Massachusetts. Then Sparrow's dad needed to paint the empty unit and do some repairs before it could be rented to a new tenant. That meant Mrs. Moon could stay right where she was until the kittens were born—which they thought would be any day now. After the kittens were weaned and given away, Sparrow and her parents would drive down to Massachusetts to deliver Mrs. Moon to Mrs. LaRose.

"And *that*," said her dad, just as Sparrow shoveled a whole twirled-up swirl into her mouth, "will be the last cat."

Wait—*what?* Sparrow didn't like the sound of that.

"But . . . ," she began, which made half the twirl slip back out of her mouth and dangle down her chin. "But

I want to talk to you guys!" Which made all the rest of the spaghetti slither back onto her plate.

"Sparrow!" said her mom. "This is what 'Don't talk with your mouth full' is all about, honey."

"Oh, not cool, Sparrow," said her dad, closing his eyes for a second, like he wished he could unsee what he had just seen.

"Sorry!" said Sparrow. "It's slippery!"

She put down her fork. It was time to make her case. "Mom. Dad. I found homes for all the cats, right? And I know I can find homes for the kittens. But can I please, please, please, please, please, please, *please* keep one of the kittens?" Holding on to the seat of her chair, she rocked side to side. Waiting for their answer.

Her mom pulled her long brown hair out from its scrunchie and twisted it back up again. Stalling. Her dad tapped his fingers on his mustache. Stalling. They were looking at each other, having one of those word-less grown-up conversations.

Mom: *You tell her.*

Dad: *No, you tell her.*

Sparrow couldn't wait much longer. *Tell me what?* Were they stalling because they were going to say no? And they didn't want a big scene? Except they were smiling at each other.

"Actually," said her mom, "your dad and I have been discussing this."

Sparrow stopped rocking side to side and held perfectly still. Hoping.

"You've shown a lot of responsibility the last few weeks," said her mom. "You really stepped up, taking care of the cats while Mrs. LaRose was in the hospital."

"And finding homes for the cats," said her dad. "That took a lot of positive energy. That was amazing. That was . . ." He stopped in midsentence, like he was searching for the right word.

"Sparrow," prompted her mom, filling in the blank. "Let's admit it, Dan. That was Sparrow being Sparrow. At her best."

"Agreed," said her dad, laughing. "That was using the power of your Sparrowness for good!"

"So," said her mom, "we're going to say *probably*—"

Sparrow jumped out of her chair, hugged her mom, hugged her dad, ran once around the table, and sat back down. "Thank you thank you thank you thank you *thank you!*"

"Listen," added her mom. "'Probably' does not mean 'definitely,' right? We don't know yet how many kittens there will be. And you promised one to Paloma, remember? So that comes first."

"I know!" said Sparrow. "But cats have more than one kitten, right?"

Her dad asked, "You know the expression 'Don't count your chickens before they hatch'? Well, this is 'Don't count your kittens before they're born.'"

"She'll have more than one," said Sparrow. "I know it!"

"It's quite possible," said her mom. "But we don't know. We'll see."

We'll see. Why did grown-ups always say "We'll see" as if all they could see were reasons something might not work out? Reasons why they would have to say no to something. Reasons why they were *not* going to make a promise. It was like they were trying to make you not get your hopes up.

Sparrow didn't care. Her hopes were up. Way, way up.

⤜ 31 ⤛

The next day at church Miss Cathy said, "Welcome back, Sunday school friends!" and Miss Lucy said, "Hey," waving and flashing a bright blue smile.

On the wall were the pictures they had made last week—their hands outlined in thick black marker and colored in. And there was a big poster of two hands pressed together in prayer, showing what each finger meant. Thumb: people closest to you. Pointer: teachers. Tallest finger: leaders. Fourth finger: people who need help. Pinky finger: yourself.

"Today—" began Miss Cathy, when there was a knock on the door.

It opened to two ladies. Behind them, kids were running up and down the hallway.

"Sorry to interrupt," said one of the ladies, "but my

helper's a no-show. Can we combine classes? I've got the fifth and sixth graders."

"I've got the kindergartners and first graders," said the second lady, "and I'd love to join too. We were going to bake, and I forgot my bag with all the ingredients."

"All the classes?" asked Miss Cathy. "You want to put a dozen kids in one of these rooms?"

"If it's okay," said the first lady.

"Or we could take them outside," suggested the second one.

Miss Cathy pressed her hands together. Sparrow wondered if she was praying for the pointer finger (teachers) or the pinky finger (herself). Probably both.

Miss Lucy gave a little wave of her hand. "I know a game! It's good for a big group. But we need a big space."

"Thank God for you, Lucy," said Miss Cathy. "All right, everyone, let's go outside."

A minute later Sparrow found herself outside with a dozen kids, running around on a grassy green lawn. At the edge of the grass stood a row of big-headed sunflowers. Lemon-yellow birds were swooping in and landing on them, then taking off into a bright blue sky.

"Huddle up!" called Miss Lucy. "And everybody needs a partner."

Sparrow looked around. From her class there was her and Anton and Hayden and Lionel and Amelia (who had cried at choir because of her dead goldfish).

From the older class there were the other choir kids: Becca and Sadie, and Daniel and Nathaniel. And there were three little kids. Anton took the hand of one of them. Becca reached for her twin sister Sadie's hand. Sparrow didn't really want to hold hands with any of the boys. She grabbed Amelia's hand, and Amelia looked up at her as if Sparrow had just said, "Time for ice cream."

"We're going to play Noah's Ark," said Miss Lucy.

"What's an ark?" asked Lionel.

Hayden began making barking noises. "Ark, ark, ark," he barked.

Other kids began barking.

"Good animal noises!" shouted Miss Lucy. "But in this game"—she lowered her voice, as if she were telling them a secret—"you have to be *totally silent*."

The barking kids stopped barking so they could hear, and Miss Lucy went on. A long time ago, there was going to be a gigantic flood. It was going to rain for so long that water was going to cover the whole earth. God told Noah to build an ark—a huge boat—and to bring two of every animal species onto the ark. It was to save them from going extinct. If they didn't get on the ark, they would drown. But God wanted to save them.

"Now here's the game," said Miss Lucy. "I'm going to whisper to each pair of you what species of animal you are. Then you're going to pretend to be that animal, getting onto the ark, and we have to guess what you are. But you have to show us *silently*, just by the way you move, without making any noise. Got it?"

"Oh, Lucy," said Miss Cathy. She wasn't pressing her hands together in prayer anymore. "That is genius."

Two by two, kids crossed the grassy space, heading toward the make-believe ark of the picnic table. Anton and his partner walked bent over, swinging one arm in front of them. Elephants! Becca and Sadie trotted and cantered and galloped around. Horses! There were flying eagles and slithering snakes and lumbering bears.

Finally it was Sparrow's turn. She and Amelia leaned close to hear their assignment. Sparrow tried to send Miss Lucy a silent message. *Cats,* she thought. *We want to be cats.*

"Cats," whispered Miss Lucy.

Sparrow felt a little chill, like she had just taken the first lick of an ice-cream cone. Sweet! Miss Lucy was so awesome.

Now to be a cat. Amelia was watching her, ready to do anything she did. Sparrow knew that no cat would walk in a straight line from here to there. So before they padded across the grassy space, she sat and began pretending to wash her ears with her paws. Amelia did the same. Then, thinking of how Mrs. Moon liked to twine around Mrs. LaRose's legs, she began circling Miss Lucy's legs. Amelia followed. Together they circled once, then stopped and licked their paws, then circled again.

"Cat!" cried Anton. "You're cats!"

"Nailed it," said Miss Lucy. "Good job, everybody."

"Snack time!" announced Miss Cathy. "But first let's all thank Miss Lucy!" She raised both hands in the air, waving them back and forth, and all the kids and other teachers joined her in a round of silent applause. Then kids scrambled for a seat at the picnic table. Cups of apple juice and paper plates of gluten-free crackers were passed around. The grace song was sung.

"You were such a good cat, Sparrow," said Lucy. "Do you have a cat?"

"Not really," said Sparrow, nibbling a cracker. "Do you?"

"I used to," said Lucy, shaking her head. "But she went missing. She was such a great cat, too. You reminded me of her, the way you went around and around my ankles. That's exactly what she used to do!"

Sparrow started to have a funny, shivering feeling. It was sort of like the feeling when you took the first lick of an ice-cream cone. Cold. But this wasn't cold and sweet. It was cold and scared. Scared to know the rest of Lucy's story. Except she had to know.

"What color was she?"

"White," said Lucy. "All white."

⤻ 32 ⤺

Sparrow put down her paper cup of apple juice. She put down her cracker. Wrapping her arms around her middle, she rocked side to side. Her stomach hurt. It was like two feelings were having a fight in there.

The first feeling was knowing how happy it would make Miss Lucy to find the cat she had lost. The second feeling was knowing how sad it would make Mrs. LaRose to lose the cat she had found. So what were you supposed to do when the same thing would make one person happy and one person sad?

"You okay?" asked Miss Lucy.

Sparrow shook her head. "I have a stomachache," she answered, just as Miss Cathy announced it was time to go join their parents for the rest of the service.

Sparrow trooped inside with the other kids, into the sanctuary, where the sun was shining through the stained-glass windows. Spotting Mrs. LaRose's hat—a straw hat with make-believe flowers—she headed that way and slid onto the pew between her mom and Mrs. LaRose.

She felt Mrs. LaRose's elbow nudging her in the side.

"Oopsy-daisy," whispered Mrs. LaRose, pointing at something. The last page of the service leaflet. The notices: "Please join us for a festive coffee hour after the service to say goodbye to longtime parishioner Helen LaRose. Also, if you would like to adopt one of her cats, please speak to the Robinson family."

"We didn't need this after all. You already found homes for them!"

All the cats were in their new homes except Mrs. Moon. Where should her home be? Should she go to a new home, with Mrs. LaRose? Or back to her old home, with Miss Lucy? Sparrow began rocking side to side again, trying to make the stomachache feeling go away. But it wasn't going anywhere.

The organ started playing and everyone stood to sing. Her mom opened a hymnal and pointed to the song: "Amazing Grace."

Sparrow was just starting to get the hang of how musical notes were like words. You could read them. And each one meant something. Mostly she didn't like people doing things for her, but she didn't mind her mom moving her finger along the page, following the notes up and down. Together they sang:

Amazing grace! How sweet the sound

Next to her mom, her dad was singing too.

That saved a wretch like me!

On the other side of Sparrow stood Mrs. LaRose and Jenny, singing without even looking at the hymn book. They knew the words by heart. Sparrow took her eyes off the page to look up at Mrs. LaRose, and Mrs. LaRose seemed to feel Sparrow's gaze on her, because she turned to Sparrow and smiled a huge smile, like the song made her so happy.

I once was lost, but now am found,
Was blind; but now I see.

That's when Sparrow knew for sure. Mrs. Moon had been lost. Now she needed to be found. Sparrow needed to tell everyone what she knew.

When the song ended, people began filing out of the sanctuary. The service was over.

"Come on," said Mrs. LaRose, pushing her walker ahead of her. "Let's go to my party!" ·

The next few minutes were a blur. People standing around, talking and eating and drinking. Kids running around, pretending to be bears and horses and elephants. A few people made little speeches about how much they would miss Mrs. LaRose.

"And her hats," called Mrs. Randolph. "I'm going to miss those hats!"

Anton ran up to Sparrow. "Come on!" he said. "They have brownies!"

"No, thanks," said Sparrow, shaking her head.

Anton ran off, and his mom called "No running!" as the crowd divided, making way for him.

"He's like Moses," said Mrs. LaRose, "parting the sea."

"I need a little less Moses and a little more good manners," said Mrs. Randolph, going after him.

Everyone was laughing—Mrs. LaRose and Jenny LaRose and Sparrow's mom and dad—when Sparrow saw somebody coming through the space Anton had cleared. Miss Lucy, heading straight toward them.

"Hey!" she said, waving hello and flashing a big smile that showed her sky-blue braces. "I wanted to say good luck in your new place, Mrs. LaRose."

"Thank you, Lucy," said Mrs. LaRose.

Miss Lucy turned to Sparrow's parents. "And I wanted to make sure Sparrow was okay. She had a stomachache in Sunday school."

All eyes turned to Sparrow.

"Why didn't you tell me?" asked her mom. "Are you okay now? Do you need to go home?"

Sparrow shook her head. No. She didn't need to go home. She needed to make sure a lost cat could go home. She looked up at Miss Lucy. "You know how you lost your cat? I think Mrs. LaRose found her."

Everybody started talking at once. Sparrow's head went back and forth, following the questions and the answers.

She had lost her cat?

Yes, that summer.

Near Hartley Street?

Yes, right near there!

Soft? White? Very affectionate?

Yes, exactly!

Maybe Mrs. Moon wasn't moving away after all!

That was funny! They called her Mrs. Moon? Lucy had called her Luna!

Hang on. What about the kittens?

Kittens?

Kittens. Any day now. It might be best to keep Mrs. Moon where she was for now. Then Lucy could take her home after the kittens were born and weaned.

"Wait!" cried Sparrow. It seemed like everybody was so excited that they were forgetting something. She turned to Mrs. LaRose. "Now you won't have a cat. And you're a cat lady. You love cats."

Mrs. LaRose held up her hand before Sparrow's parents could scold Sparrow for calling her a cat lady. "I can't take a cat that belongs to somebody else, Sparrow. But you're right. I would like to have a cat. Maybe I can have one of the kittens."

"I have an idea," said Lucy. "What if you keep Luna—Mrs. Moon? And I take one of the kittens instead?"

Mrs. LaRose loved that idea. Jenny LaRose and Sparrow's mom and Sparrow's dad loved the idea. Even Sparrow thought it was a pretty good idea. Except for one thing. A kitten for Paloma and a kitten for Miss Lucy meant two kittens spoken for. Would there be one for her?

⤜ 33 ⤝

The next week inched forward. Breakfast with her dad. School. After school, going with Anton to his house for aftercare. Home to check on Mrs. Moon. Supper with her mom.

But the last day of the week was different. On Friday, Sparrow got to leave school early because she was going to the doctor. Not for her, though. For her mom and the baby.

Her mom picked her up and they drove for a while.

"So, how's school going?" asked her mom.

"Okay."

"Are you and Paloma all made up?"

"Pretty much," answered Sparrow, because she was back to being friends with Paloma. But just like she'd been afraid of, Paloma wanted to stay friends with Anna, too. She wanted the three of them to sit together at lunch and hang out together at recess. Which wasn't easy for Sparrow.

"Being friends doesn't always go smoothly, does it?" asked her mom. "Sometimes there's some up-and-down bumps. Are you two in a bumpy place?"

Surprised, Sparrow nodded yes. Her mom knew how she felt? And she wasn't trying to talk her out of it? Or telling her what to do? Instead her mom just made a little murmuring noise, like she understood.

"How about aftercare at Anton's?" asked her mom. "How's that going?"

"It's okay," said Sparrow. "It's not too bad."

"I bet you miss your afternoons with Mrs. LaRose," said her mom as she pulled into a parking lot ringed with tall trees.

Sparrow nodded again.

Her mom turned off the car. "Well, I'm really glad you wanted to come along this afternoon."

"Um, okay," said Sparrow as they got out and headed toward a tall brick building.

She wouldn't exactly say she *wanted* to go to her mom's doctor appointment. But her mom had seemed so excited about the idea. Like it was a big deal. Like it would be fun. Sparrow wasn't so sure, but she had figured it was better than being in school and going to aftercare. She didn't want to say that, though. She didn't want to hurt her mom's feelings.

"That's okay," said her mom. "I don't mind if you just came because you wanted to leave school early and skip aftercare."

Sparrow felt a surge of relief sink into her. Like when you were hot and thirsty, and you took a slug of icy-cold lemonade. Lots of times she felt like her mom didn't understand why she said what she said or did what she did. But today it felt like her mom could see inside her. And her mom wasn't trying to fix what she saw. And suddenly, right there on the walkway outside the doctor's, her mom opened her arms and Sparrow stepped into them for a hug. All around them, the trees' yellow

and orange and red leaves were swishing in the blue sky.

Inside, the doctor's office was full of people waiting for their turn. Ladies who were having babies, sitting in chairs. A couple of toddlers, crawling around a play area. A couple of dads. Sparrow and her mom sat down to wait too. In a while she heard her mom's name being called. "Susan Robinson?" It was their turn.

"Welcome!" said the doctor as they squeezed into a little room. She had long black hair that ran in a single braid down the back of her long white coat. "Good to see you again, Susan. And you must be Sparrow! I'm Dr. Beth. Are you here to get a look at your baby?"

Sparrow didn't like to answer stupid questions. This wasn't *her* baby. She knew it was rude not to answer, though, so she was trying to think of something to say when her mom answered for her. Usually that made her mad. Because usually her mom said what she thought Sparrow *should* say, which was not what Sparrow really felt. But not today. Today her mom nailed it.

"Sparrow would probably rather take a look at the babies we have at our house. We're taking care of a cat who's about to have kittens."

"Kittens?" cried Dr. Beth. "You lucky duck! When I was a kid, my cat had kittens. It was so exciting! I honestly think that's one of the reasons I became a doctor."

"Did you get to see them being born?" asked Sparrow.

"No," said Dr. Beth. "I didn't see them until they were

a few hours old. But that was probably best. Cats are different than people. A mama cat can do the job herself, and she would probably rather do it alone."

The whole time Dr. Beth was talking, she was doing things with Sparrow's mom. She listened to her heart with a stethoscope. She wrapped a cuff around her arm and took her blood pressure.

Then Dr. Beth held up something that looked kind of like a big mouse for a computer. "This is a transducer. It's going to show us how the baby is doing. Ready to take a look?"

"Okay," said Sparrow, glad that Dr. Beth had stopped saying "your baby."

Sparrow's mom lay down, and Dr. Beth squirted some goop onto her bare stomach. "How far along is she? The mama cat, I mean."

"We're not sure," answered Sparrow's mom. "But she's big. We think any day now."

"Exciting!" said Dr. Beth. She put the big mouse thing on Sparrow's mom's stomach and began sliding it around in circles. "That would mean that those kittens are just about the size of . . ." Suddenly she stopped in the middle of what she was saying. She stopped moving the mouse thing. She said in a soft voice, "This little person."

Sparrow heard a sound. *Glub-glub. Glub-glub.* Her mom grabbed her hand and gave it a squeeze.

"Can you hear the heartbeat?" asked Dr. Beth.

Sparrow and her mom were both nodding, together. Sparrow's mom was still squeezing her hand, squishing it. Sparrow didn't mind. She was squeezing back. *Glub-glub. Glub-glub.*

The mouse thing was attached to a screen, which Dr. Beth pulled closer. "And can you see this shape here?" she asked, pointing to the screen. "That's your baby brother."

That made sense. It wasn't *her* baby. But it *was* her baby brother.

"He's so *little*," said Sparrow.

"Well," said Dr. Beth, "he still has some growing to do before he's born. Human babies take a lot longer to develop than kittens. But everything looks good."

"You want to be the one to tell your dad?" asked Sparrow's mom.

"Tell him what?"

"That the baby looks healthy, and that we're having a boy."

Sparrow couldn't believe it. *She knew before her dad?* "Daddy doesn't know?"

"No, because I just found out right now, with you. That's why I wanted you to come along."

"Sure!" said Sparrow. "I'll tell him."

They listened to the *glub-glub* sound a little longer and watched the tiny shape. It was weird to hear and see something that was *inside* her mom. But her mom had been able to tell things that were inside of Sparrow. How being friends wasn't always easy for her. How much she missed Mrs. LaRose. How excited she was about the kittens. But now she was kind of excited about the baby, too.

After the appointment her mom drove them home. Sparrow went inside to get the key to Mrs. LaRose's unit. "I'm going to check on Mrs. Moon," she told her mom.

"Good to know," said her mom.

Sparrow walked across the long front porch and put the key in the lock of Mrs. LaRose's door. She remembered how weird it had felt, the first time she went in there, all alone. Now she was used to it. Some things were different. Most of the furniture was gone, and the house had an empty feeling. But some things were the same. The old-fashioned phone was still stuck to the wall. The tall grandfather clock still stood in its spot, because there wasn't room for it where Mrs. LaRose had gone to live.

It was so quiet that Sparrow could hear the ticking of the clock as she padded down the hall to the living room. The room was empty except for the cat bed in one corner, where Mrs. Moon lay stretched out on the bed's pillow. Nursing her kittens.

Sparrow knew she shouldn't touch them. Not yet.

She shouldn't even get too close. But she could get close
enough to see that they were all black-and-white. And
close enough to see how many "all" was.

One. Two. Three. One for Paloma. One for Miss Lucy.
One for her.

I'm going to be honest with you. I didn't see this story with my own eyes. The whole thing happened before I was born. And even after I was born, for a little while I couldn't see. But that's normal for cats. We're born with our eyes closed, and in a couple of weeks they open. Sparrow told me everything, though. From the day she knocked over Mrs. LaRose and broke her hip . . .

. . . until the day my eyes opened and I could see for myself. It was the first Sunday in October, a little over a week after I was born. The Sparrow family had gone to the Blessing of the Animals. I would have liked to go, but I was still too young. Sparrow says I can go next year for sure.

The service began outside, on the grassy space where the kids had played the Noah's ark game. The yellow sun was shining on the yellow sunflowers. Their heads were so heavy with seeds now that they were drooping facedown. There were dogs on leashes. Cats in carrying cases. A bunny in a cage. A hamster.

My mom stayed home with us kittens, but some of her old housemates were there. Midnight, with Anton and his mom and aunt. Pierre and Paulette with Mr. Parker, the choir director.

Everybody milled around on the grass, and the pastor went around saying a blessing to each animal. The children's choir sang a song. The whole thing was really nice.

After church, when she and Mr. and Mrs. Sparrow got home, Sparrow came hurrying in, and that's when I saw her for the first time. While they'd been at the service, my eyes had opened.

I saw that she had brown eyes. Light brown hair. Red-brown freckles sprinkled on white skin. But mostly what I saw was a big smile that lit up her face. She was so excited to see me! Later I learned that her parents say she can get a little too excited sometimes. Carried away. That's just Sparrow, though. Sparrow being Sparrow. And it's fine by me.

You can probably figure out the rest of the story. My sister went to live with a nice kid named Paloma, who wears kitty-cat headbands, so you know she loves cats. My brother went to live with a teenage girl named Lucy. My mom lives in Massachusetts now, with Mrs. LaRose. And I got to stay with Sparrow.

She named me Grace. Actually, she got a little carried away naming me, so my full name is Amazing Grace

LaRose. Sparrow says my name is half because I am just plain so amazing and half from the song.

Amazing grace! How sweet the sound
That saved a wretch like me!
I once was lost, but now am found,
Was blind, but now I see.

I do feel like Sparrow found me. Like she loves me, and I'm home now. I hope she feels the same about me. That I love her, and she's home. She says I'm amazing, but I think she is. I guess we're a good pair.

⤳ ACKNOWLEDGMENTS ⤦

I am grateful to the writers who helped shape Sparrow's story into a book—Charlotte Agell, Maria Padian, Debra Spark, Elizabeth Searle, and Ann Harleman with her "golden red pen."

Gail Donovan was fired from her first job in an ice cream shop for making the sundaes too big. She now works in a library and writes middle-grade novels, including the Moonbeam Children's Book Award winner *Finchosaurus* and *In Memory of Gorfman T. Frog*, named to the New York Public Library's 100 Books for Reading and Sharing list. She has also written for the Rainbow Fish & Friends picture book series based on the bestselling work of Marcus Pfister. Donovan lives on the coast of Maine, where she jumps in the ocean all year round. She has shared her home with a dozen birds, a few dogs, a rat, and a cat named Cookie.

Elysia Case is an illustrator from the Finger Lakes region of New York. When she's not making things, she can be found spoiling her pets with too many treats and annoying them with too many kisses.